KU-033-344

Catherine Cookson was born in Tyne Dock and the place of her birth provides the background she so vividly creates in many of her novels. Although acclaimed as a regional writer – her novel THE ROUND TOWER won the Winifred Holtby Award for the best regional novel of 1968 – her readership spreads throughout the world. Her work has been translated into twelve languages and Corgi alone has 40,000,000 copies of her novels in print, including those written under the name of Catherine Marchant.

Mrs Cookson was born the illegitimate daughter of a poverty-stricken woman, Kate, whom she believed to be her older sister. Catherine began work in service but eventually moved south to Hastings where she met and married a local grammar school master. At the age of forty she began writing with great success about the lives of the working class people of the North-East with whom she had grown up, including her intriguing autobiography, OUR KATE. Her many bestselling novels have established her as one of the most popular of contemporary women novelists.

Mrs Cookson now lives in Northumberland.

Other books by Catherine Cookson

and published by Corgi Books

Catherine Cookson

The Lord and Mary Ann

CORGI BOOKS

THE LORD AND MARY ANN

A CORGI BOOK   0 552 08822 6

Originally published in Great Britain
by Macdonald & Co. (Publishers) Ltd

PRINTING HISTORY

Macdonald edition published 1956
Corgi edition published 1971
Corgi edition reprinted 1972
Corgi edition reprinted 1973
Corgi edition reprinted 1974
Corgi edition reprinted 1976
Corgi edition reprinted 1977
Corgi edition reprinted 1978
Corgi edition reprinted 1979
Corgi edition reprinted 1980
Corgi edition reprinted 1981
Corgi edition reprinted 1985
Corgi edition reprinted 1986
Corgi edition reprinted 1988

Copyright © Catherine Cookson 1956

Conditions of sale:
1. This book is sold subject to the condition that it shall not,
by way of trade *or otherwise*, be lent, re-sold, hired out or
otherwise *circulated* without the publisher's prior consent in
any form of binding or cover other than that in which it is
published *and without a similar condition including this condition
being imposed on the subsequent purchaser.*
2. This book is sold subject to the Standard Conditions of
Sale of Net Books and may not be re-sold in the U.K. below
the net price fixed by the publishers for the book.

This book is set in 10 pt. Intertype Baskerville

Corgi Books are published by Transworld Publishers Ltd.,
61–63 Uxbridge Road, Ealing, London W5 5SA,
in Australia by Transworld Publishers (Australia) Pty. Ltd.,
15–23 Helles Avenue, Moorebank, NSW 2170, and in New
Zealand by Transworld Publishers (N.Z.) Ltd., Cnr. Moselle
and Waipareira Avenues, Henderson, Auckland.

Printed and bound in Great Britain by
Hazell Watson & Viney Limited
Member of BPCC plc
Aylesbury, Bucks, England

CONTENTS

CHAPTER ONE

A RESPECTABLE COW

THE cowshed was full. It was full of cows and activity, of pails clanging, of noises like jets of escaping steam, of deep lowings, of snuffles and swishes, of hooves meeting stone, of steaming flesh, and contentment. Mike Shaughnessy leaned his head against the warm, brown skin. His brow moved gently over a rib, and the cow, a dappled Jersey, turned a deeply soft eye on him. Her jaws moved twice; she turned away again and let her milk run freely.

'Mike.'

'Aye?' He did not turn his head from the beast's side, but screwed it round to look at the man who was addressing him.

'It's rainin' again. What d'you bet he doesn't send you out to the top field?'

Mike lifted his head and looked full at the undersized man who, hose in hand, was directing a jet of water along the gutter flanking the byres.

'Well, if he does, what of it?'

The other man stared for a moment before saying, 'Why, man, I can't understand you. You're a damn fool. What d'you put up with it for? When it's wet you're out, when it's fine you're in. He gives you all the muck. You'll never get the tractor through that bog.'

'I'll try. And look, Jonesy' – Mike stood up, and his height and breadth dwarfed the man still further – 'it's like this: if I don't make a hullabaloo about it I don't see any reason why you should. So don't keep on.'

'You needn't take it like that. I'm not keeping on. But what I maintain is, if he does it to one he's just as likely to do it to another. .... I'd like to see him try it on me. I was engaged for one job. I don't even mind doin' two or three,

7

but I wouldn't stand for what he dishes out to you. Aw, man,' Jones leaned towards Mike, and continued quietly, 'why don't you tell him to go to hell? What can he do to you but give you the sack?'

'Da.'

Both men turned, and Jones, his manner jovial now, said, 'Hallo there, Mary Ann.'

'Hallo, Mr. Jones.'

Mary Ann looked at the farmhand. She wasn't sure, even after having known Mr. Jones for three months, whether she liked him or not. Sometimes he made her laugh . . . but not when he was talking to her da.

She turned to Mike, saying, 'Me ma says, are you comin'? Your breakfast's been ready for ages.'

'I'll be there in a minute.' Mike lifted the brimming pail, and Jones said, 'Give it here, I'll see to it. You should be comin' back now 'stead of goin'.'

Mike handed over the pail and with no further words left the cowshed, Mary Ann walking somewhat soberly by his side.

'Da, can we have a dog?'

'What do you want a dog for? There's two on the farm already, and you've got Tibby.'

'I know, but a cat's not a dog. And Mr. Ratcliffe doesn't like us to play with the farm dogs.'

'Well, we'll see,' said Mike.

'Da—' The inflexion Mary Ann now gave to the word told Mike that whatever was to follow was of grave importance.

'Aye, what is it?' he said.

'Isn't a heifer a bull?'

One side of Mike's mouth pulled up, but restraining his smile he said, 'Hardly that.'

'But it is, Da.' Mary Ann paused in her walk to add emphasis to this statement.

But when Mike continued to move steadily on she ran and caught him up and pulled at his hand. 'But it is, Da. It must be.'

'Well, if you say it is, it is.'

They continued across the yard in silence, and out on to the road. Away over the fields the rain looked like a swaying

8

sheet let down from the surrounding fells. Even the knowledge that the weather looked set and that in a very short time he would be out working in it did not affect Mike adversely. Each day was good, for his feet were on the ground. No longer did he have to listen to the banging and hammering of the shipyard; no longer climb the gantries and tremble at their height; no longer was he hemmed in by people, people as thickly packed as the bricks in the walls of their houses. He was in the open once again doing the job he was created for. He had no religious beliefs, had Mike, but of this he was sure: each man had been made for a specific purpose, and his was to tend animals and to work under the open sky. Time and again he had tried it, only to be driven back to the towns and the yards. But now he was settled – thanks to this mite.

He put out his hand and grasped his daughter's, and this to Mary Ann was the signal that her da didn't want to be quiet any longer and that he wouldn't mind if she chattered. So once again she pressed her point regarding the sex of a heifer.

'It must be a bull, Da.'

Mike's head suddenly went back in its old carefree fashion and his laugh ran along the hedges like wind and sent the birds into a chirruping and a chittering. Mary Ann, too, was forced into laughter, and she pulled on his hand, saying, 'Oh Da, give over and tell me – come on. Aw!'

'Look' – Mike nodded along the road – 'there's your mother. I'm in for it.'

Elizabeth Shaughnessy was standing by the cottage gate. She was a tall, blonde woman, as tall as her husband, and with a carriage that had something of defiance in its straightness. Mary Ann looked along the road towards her, and, as oft-times happened, she was so struck by the beauty of her mother's face that all else was sent spinning from her mind. She had always considered her ma bonnie, even when they were living in the attics in Mulhattan's Hall and her da had got sick at times and didn't come home with his pay, when her ma's face would become drawn and her voice sharp. Even then she had remained bonnie. But since they'd come to the farm the word bonnie no longer fitted her, for now she was beautiful, and she laughed with her da and they

9

larked on in the kitchen at nights. Even their Michael was happy and all swanky now that he was at the Grammar School.

The wonder of life shot through Mary Ann, and she leapt clean off the road and with a shout dashed to the gate and to Elizabeth.

'Now look, stop it! What's come over you? Don't go mad. Go on, start your breakfast or you'll miss the bus.' Lizzie pushed Mary Ann up the path, then turned to greet her husband: 'You get later . . . anything wrong?'

'Wrong? What could be wrong?' He paused a moment and looked into her eyes, which were on a level with his own. 'Why can't you stop worrying?'

She sighed and smiled quietly. 'Come on, have your breakfast.'

Midst the warm smell of fried bacon they sat down: Mike and Elizabeth on one side of the table, Michael and Mary Ann on the other.

Michael ate hurriedly, his eyelids blinking as his thoughts darted to and fro in his mind.

'Don't gollop your food,' Lizzie cautioned him, and Mary Ann, crunching a crisp piece of bacon rind, added slyly, 'He's hurrying to get to the bus stop to meet Lena Ratcliffe.'

'I'm not! I'm not!' His face scarlet, and almost choking on his food, Michael glared at Mary Ann.

'Yes, you are; you both talk swanky.' She now proceeded to pull her nose down and lengthen her upper lip until it completely covered her lower one, whilst she mimicked, 'My form mistress . . . my form master.'

'You—' Michael was on his feet.

'Sit down. Sit down.' Mike's voice was gentle to his son. But to his beloved daughter his voice took on a sternness: 'And you get on with your breakfast if you don't want your backside skelped.'

Mary Ann took this threat for what it was worth. Her head wagged, and she continued her breakfast in hurt silence. And in the quiet that followed, her thoughts returned to the troublesome problem that must be straightened out before she went to school. She must make quite sure that a heifer was a bull, for as soon as she should set her foot in the school yard this morning Sarah Flannagan would start again trying to be clever and making on she knew everything.

This time she appealed to her mother, saying, 'Ma, isn't a heifer a baby bull?'

Lizzie almost looked startled. 'A baby . . .?' She did not finish but glanced towards Mike. But Mike was very intent on his breakfast.

'A baby bull?' Michael's voice now was full of scorn. 'You're daft!'

'It is! It is!' Mary Ann attacked him.

'Now stop that shouting,' Lizzie cautioned her, 'and go and wash your hands.'

'But, Ma, isn't it? I must tell Sarah Flannagan.'

Mary Ann's face looked full of misery.

'But why do you want to tell Sarah that?' asked Lizzie.

'Because she talks potty,' said Mary Ann. 'She says it isn't a bull, she says it's nothing. She says her ma says it becomes a cow when it gets married.'

There was a great spluttering and choking. Mike had been in the act of drinking his last mouthful of tea; now most of it sprayed across the table. Rising swiftly, he went into the scullery.

Mary Ann watched the scullery door until he reappeared. He was red in the face. 'I'm afraid Sarah's got one on you this time,' he said.

'But, Da—'

'Now, now, it's no use arguing that point. Sarah's right.'

'Aw, but—'

'Look. Get your hands washed this minute!'

And Lizzie enforced this command by pushing Mary Ann from the table towards the scullery. Then her glance met Mike's, and her silent laughter joined his.

'Trust Nellie Flannagan,' said Mike, under his breath, 'to bring the sanctity of marriage to a cow.'

Lizzie walked with Mary Ann to the gate. Her daughter was looking anything but pleased – the fact that Sarah had scored over her had the power to darken her sky, and, incidentally, to put her in a fighting mood. If Mary Ann's retaliation could be directed solely against Sarah this morning, Lizzie would not have felt the slightest qualm. But before Mary Ann would meet Sarah she would meet Lena, and the farm manager's daughter had in an odd way assumed the embodiment of a threat to the family's new-found security. She wanted at this moment to bend down and grasp hold of Mary Ann's hand and beg of her, 'Be nice to Lena, will you? And don't brag about Mr. Lord.'

As if Mary Ann had heard the echo of Mr. Lord's name, she looked up at her mother and said, 'If the Lord – I mean Mr. Lord – comes afore the bus he'll take us into Jarrow, and if he does can I spend me bus fare, Ma?'

'No,' said Lizzie, buttoning up the collar of Mary Ann's mackintosh. 'You've done that twice this week already. It's to go into your money-box. Don't forget Christmas isn't so far off. And Mary Ann–' Lizzie paused and adjusted the round school hat.

'Yes, Ma?'

'Don't be cheeky to Lena, will you?'

The stark injustice of this remark widened Mary Ann's brown eyes and brought her mouth to a button.

'I'm not, Ma. She's cheeky to me, and always swanking. She's—'

'All right! All right! Only I'm telling you. And pay heed. Go on now.' Lizzie kissed the pained face, then with a push sent Mary Ann on her way down the lane. She watched her until she reached the bend, and when the child turned and gave a desultory wave she waved back, then went thoughtfully into the cottage.

The bus stop was at the crossroads and was indicated by a heap of gravel lying by the side of the road at the foot of a signpost, one arm of which pointed to Gateshead and the other to Shields. At the far side of the gravel stood Lena Ratcliffe, a thick-set yet tall girl of eleven. Her hair was brown and fluffy, and her face could have been pretty had it not shown so much petulance. Michael was standing somewhat self-consciously in front of the heap and Mary Ann on the near side. Each was constrained. Mary Ann, not because of the presence of the other two, but because once again she had been put in the wrong. . . . Her ma saying, 'Don't be cheeky to Lena! She had never been half as cheeky to Lena as she had wanted to be. If she'd done all the things she'd wanted to do to Lena her ma might have room to talk. She often wanted to butt her in the stomach, or knock her into the big pig trough.

But the thought of Lena vanished as a large black car turned the bend and moved swiftly towards them. Simultaneously the two girls stepped on to the road. Mary Ann said nothing, only her eyes widened and her face took on a look of happy expectancy, not unmixed with self-satisfied propriety.

As the car drew to a halt, Lena, with studied dignity, went to the window and said, 'Good morning, Mr. Lord. May I sit in the front?'

Mr. Lord did not return the greeting. His brows were beetling over the top of his eyes, shadowing the deep blue to black, his white moustache was bristling on his pursed upper lip, and his whole attitude expressed barely controlled rage.

'Get in the back.'

With a sound like. 'Huh!' Lena opened the door and climbed into the back seat.

Michael, who was standing behind Mary Ann, said respectfully and a little apprehensively, 'Good morning, sir.'

' 'Morning. Get in.'

Michael got in and sat beside Lena.

With the air of a duchess taking her rightful place, Mary Ann now opened the front door of the car and wriggled herself on to the seat.

'Hallo!' She grinned at the old man – the Lord, as she always thought of him.

He cast a swift sidelong glance at her. A light gleamed in the shadows of his eyes for a moment; his moustache moved, and he muttered something that could have been 'Hallo!'

As the car bounded forward, Lena placed her head between Mary Ann and Mr. Lord, and in her politest tone, which was saying a great deal, she said, 'It's very kind of you to take us into Jarrow, Mr. Lord. Mammy says we do appreciate it.'

Mr. Lord's shoulder jerked, and Mary Ann, making an imperceptible movement nearer to him, forced Lena to remove her head. She glanced up at him, wondering if he appreciated the move she had made. But he was intent on his driving; and just as her father's silence often warned her when to keep her tongue quiet, her quick perception bade her to do so now.

Lena, in her condescending prim way, was talking to Michael, and for quite some distance the one-sided conversation centred around school. There she goes again, thought Mary Ann, always swanking . . . and he wants to be quiet. He'll go for her. I hope he does.

Her own silence gave her a definite feeling of superiority, which would have continued for the remainder of the journey had not Lena changed her topic to one which annoyed her more than did the described glories of the high school. Lena was once again mesmerising Michael with the splendour of the big house she had lived in before coming north. It was a lovely house, she was saying, big and white, with japonica all round.

Mary Ann's self-denial was weighed and found wanting. Mr. Lord's unspoken demand for quiet could not stand up to the desire to do a bit of swanking on her own account, so she screwed herself round, bringing her chin to the top of the seat.

'Us used to live in a big house an' all,' she said. She ignored the flushed face of her brother and his look which was plainly saying, 'Shut up, you fool.'

Mulhattan's Hall and the garrets at the top in which they had lived were still painfully clear in Michael's mind, and try as he might he could not wholly remove the dread of returning there.

Staring coldly back at Mary Ann, and with cutting correctness and ignoring the subject-matter of the conversation, Lena said, 'You shouldn't say "Us used to"; you should say "We used to".'

Now it was Mary Ann's turn to colour. But if she was aware of her facial betrayal she ignored it, and replied with a well-feigned airiness, even adding emphasis, 'It was us – me da and ma, and me and our Michael.'

'Be quiet, and don't be so soft!'

Michael's censorious tone brought her battling to her knees. She might have to be civil to Lena Ratcliffe, but their Michael was a different kettle of fish.

'You! – Who d'you think—?'

'Sit down this minute!'

The thunder of Mr. Lord's voice shut off her own as if with a switch. Slowly she slipped into a sitting position again, and into the purring silence came Lena's polite tones, this time addressed directly to Mr. Lord. 'It is "We used to", isn't it, Mr. Lord?' And to Mary Ann's utter astonishment, amazement, indignation and mystification, Mr. Lord answered quietly but also with emphasis, 'Yes, it is . . . "We used to".'

After staring at Mr. Lord's stiff profile for almost a quarter of a mile Mary Ann looked ahead again. He had said that! He had taken Lena Ratcliffe's part, even though he didn't like her. Without any proof but that of her intuition, she knew this. Mr. Lord was hers. He might be the owner of a shipyard and run the farm as a hobby; he might be the man whom people were afraid of; but he had given her da a job when she had gone to him and asked him even though he had refused this to Father Owen and had once sacked her da from his yard.

It was when her ma had been going to leave her da, after their Michael had tried to gas himself, that she had got up in the dark and gone right out into the country and squeezed under the barbed wire round Mr. Lord's great house and knocked on his door. And the old servant had wanted to throw her out and had told the Lord she was loopy because she had said that the Holy Family had sent her to tell him what a grand man her da was with cows and things. Mr. Lord had taken a bit of convincing, but he had given her da the job after she had made him laugh.

She liked to make him laugh – he had nobody to make him laugh, stuck in that big house all on his own. And what was more, he always believed everything she said; not like Sarah Flannagan and Lena Ratcliffe and their Michael, and even her ma and da at times. Even these last two, in varying degrees, doubted her word; but never Mr. Lord. She had even told Sarah Flannagan in front of him that he was her granda, and he had believed her. He was hers.

The car came to a stop and Michael got out, saying in an awkward fashion, 'Thank you, sir.'

Mr. Lord nodded abruptly and drove on. The car stopped again, but Lena did nothing so common as get out. She alighted, definitely pleased with herself, and said, 'Thank you so much, Mr. Lord. And goodbye.'

Again Mr. Lord nodded and drove on. And yet again he stopped. This time he leant across Mary Ann and opened the door.

Without glancing at him, she slid off the seat and on to the pavement, then turned a pained, blank countenance towards him.

'Ta.'

'Don't say "Ta", say "Thank you".'

Mary Ann's eyes popped.

Mr. Lord's brows, like miniature sweeping brushes, moved up and down as he glared at the small elfin figure on the pavement. 'Don't you know when to use "us" and "we"? What do they teach you at school?'

Closing her mouth and trying to still its trembling, she muttered, 'Sums and things.'

'Don't they teach you grammar?'

'Yes.'

'Then don't say "us" when it should be "we".'

They stared at each other, the very small girl and the tall, bristling old man. Then, swinging round, Mary Ann darted like a rabbit up the street towards the school gate. And if she heard him call her name she took no heed . . . she was hurt and bewildered, she wanted to go to the lavatory and cry and cry. But this solace was denied her, for waiting for her, together with a number of cronies, was Sarah Flannagan, and the change in sex of a heifer had to be faced and somehow got over.

It had been an awful day. Sarah Flannagan had crowed about the heifer during the two playtimes, even going as far as to produce a book which said that a heifer was a young cow. And Miss Thompson had been awful, too; she was always awful; she was even worse than Miss Johnson, and had never been impressed by the grandness of her da or his new job, or the cottage, or even Mr. Lord. And if knowing Mr. Lord didn't make people sit up and take notice of you, nothing would.

Mary Ann closed her desk and marched out with the others to the cloak-room. There, her best friend, Cissie

Bailey, told her that she would be unable to set her to the bus stop as she had to go straight home and mind the baby 'cos her ma was going in to Shields. And when her next best friend, Agnes Wilkins, said she couldn't come either because she had to go home and have her shoes mended, the world for Mary Ann became dull, almost dead. She'd have to walk the length of three long streets without an admiring audience – all her grandiose thoughts would be wasted!

She turned from them in a huff and marched away, determined never to speak to either of them again . . . and after her sharing her taffee with them an' all!

The need for Cissie's and Agnes's support became more apparent as she passed through the school gateway, for there, waiting for her, was Sarah with three of her friends. Against all rules, they remained silent as she passed them with her chin cocked in the air. And even when she had gone some distance they didn't shout after her, which was most unusual. Her curiosity forced her to look round. Although they weren't calling they were following her, and Sarah's dark, vicious face had a leer on it that Mary Ann knew portended no good. Nevertheless, she could not resist the opportunity of showing that lot, and Sarah in particular, that she wasn't afraid of them. And she did so by sticking out her tongue and wagging it violently.

This indeed was the signal for retaliation, and it came in the form of a chant, Sarah's voice being louder than the others':

> 'Swanky Shaughnessy – there she goes:
> Two boss eyes and turned-in toes;
> She cannot even wipe her nose.
> Swanky Shaughnessy – there she goes!'

Mary Ann's gait became dignified. The serpent of pride slithered round inside her – it was nice to be called swanky. But it was usual, of course, to deny it strongly, saying, 'I'm not! I'm not!' And this would be accompanied by a bobbing of the head. But on this occasion she did not retort; she was alone against four, and she was wise enough to know how far she could go. It would have been different had Cissie or Agnes been with her; then she could have revelled in the battle of tongues.

Suddenly the swanky feeling disappeared, swept away by Sarah's voice alone chanting:

> 'Pig's belly,
> Wobble jelly;
> Pig's fat,
> Dirty cat;
> Pig's skin,
> Double chin;
> Pig's cheek,
> Shiny beak;
> Pig's lug,
> Ugly mug—
> And that's Mary Ann Shaughnessy!'

Oh . . . h! Her lips were pursed, and her face was wearing its tightest buttoned-up look. Just wait, she'd let her have it. Wait till the bus was just going so she couldn't get at her, and she'd yell, 'Pig's snout, you great big lout!'

She turned into the street where the bus stop was, and Sarah and her cronies were for the moment wiped from her mind, for there, standing near the lamp post, was Lena Ratcliffe. She was staring at the back of Mitchell's factory wall. Lena never caught the bus at this stop, she caught it near the cemetery. What was she doing here? Perhaps she had to go a message. Mary Ann was overcome with an uneasiness quite inexplicable to herself. But she knew she did not want Lena Ratcliffe to meet Sarah Flannagan, so, forming her own rearguard action, she turned on the advancing girls.

'Go on. Stop following me.'

'Huh! Listen to her,' said Sarah. 'Who d'you think you are? Is it your street now?'

'I'll tell me da on you, mind.'

'Ho! ho! ho!, Sarah bellowed derisively. 'I'll tell me da! Did you hear her? I'll tell me da! Her da!'

Boiling inwardly, Mary Ann was forced to move on, until she came up to Lena. Lena was still staring at the wall on which there was some large writing in red and white chalk. But becoming aware of Mary Ann, she turned and looked down on her, and her expression was puzzling, for it was triumphant and very like Sarah Flannagan's when she had scored a victory.

Lena said nothing, no word of greeting, but slowly she looked at the wall again. Mary Ann's eyes were drawn to it, and with sagging jaw she read: 'MARY ANN SHAUGHNESSY IS A BIG LIAR AND HER DA'S A DRUNKEN NO-GOOD AND EVERYBODY KNOWS IT.'

The new life seemed to drain from Mary Ann's body as she stood gazing at the large chalked words, and the old life crept back, making her shiver – the old life she knew before they went to the farm to live, the life that was full of sickness and fear.

It was not because Sarah had written that she was a big liar, and it was not the first time that Sarah had called her da a drunken no-good, but it was because Lena had read it. Her mother's voice came to her with that strange quality it had held this morning when she said, 'Don't be cheeky to Lena.' It was as if her ma was afraid. Of what, Mary Ann could not exactly explain, yet it was to do with Lena, or her mother, or her father – and her own da.

A hot sick feeling of anxiety filled her. If anything should happen to her da. . . . If he should lose his job, and all through Sarah Flannagan. . . . Suddenly the anxiety and fear fled before a wave of fury which seemed to animate every inch of her. She turned to where Sarah was standing in the gutter grinning, and she leapt at her, tearing at her hair with her hands and using her feet against the taller girl's shins. For a moment, Sarah was taken off her guard. But it was only for a moment. She struck out and slapped Mary Ann such a ringing blow across the ear that Mary Ann's anger was knocked completely out of her, together with her wind. Her feet left the ground, and she found herself lying where Sarah had been standing.

Sarah was now on the pavement, being comforted by her friends. There was a deep scratch down the length of her cheek, and her face was dark with both pain and anger. She glared down at Mary Ann and cried, 'I'll get you wrong for this, so I will. Wait till I tell me ma. And your da isn't any good . . . he is a drunk, a great big drunk! And me ma says she gives him six months in that job afore he's thrown out;

and you'll all be glad to come crawling back to Mulhattan's Hall!'

On this enlightening tirade, Sarah flung round, and together with her cronies marched off. From a sitting position Mary Ann watched them. No one of them seemed to be walking straight; nothing was straight, the houses, the pavement ... or Lena. .... And Lena had heard.

The fury was gone, and her mind was once again full of the dark foreboding. It did not lessen as she pulled herself to her feet and looked towards the disdainful girl coldly surveying her. With a definite look of pleading in her eyes, and in an almost humble voice, Mary Ann said, 'You don't believe her, do you, Lena – what she said about me da – what's on the wall? Cos me da doesn't drink, he never even goes into a bar. You've never seen him go into the village bar, have you?'

She waited for an answer. But Lena's only reply was to lift her chin and to shrug her shoulders.

The bus came round the corner. Mary Ann watched Lena move to the edge of the kerb and stick her arm straight out. She looked down at her own hands, all mud, and at her coat and stockings, thick with dirt. If she went home like this her ma would get out of her what had happened, and she'd be upset.

The bus stopped, and Lena got on, but Mary Ann stood where she was. It wasn't even any satisfaction to her to witness Lena's surprised expression through the window as the bus moved off without her.

For quite some time Mary Ann stood, her fingers trying to still her trembling lips. Then she thought of Mrs. McBride. She would go to her ... Mrs. McBride would clean her up.

'Did you wallop her?' asked Mrs. McBride.

'I scratched her face.'

'Well, I hope it was a good long scratch.'

Fanny McBride held up Mary Ann's coat, saying, 'Don't worry, it'll soon be as good as new. Go and wash your hands and knees, then have a sup of tea, an' you'll feel your old self again.'

'Me da won't lose his job cos Lena knows, will he?'

Mrs. McBride let out a disdainful laugh which shook her

fat and made the myriad wrinkles on her face quiver. 'Lose his job? I should say not! And after Mr. Lord taking such a fancy to you.'

'Sarah said we'd have to come back here and live.'

'Not on your life. That 'un's like her mother, her venom would poison a rattlesnake. Anyway' – Fanny turned on Mary Ann – 'where's that old spunk of yours? Surely if you could manage Sarah Flannagan and Mr. Lord, you're a match enough for this Lena, or whoever she is.'

'But her da's me da's boss, and he doesn't like him very much.'

'Who? Your da or his boss?'

'Mr. Ratcliffe doesn't like me da.'

'Who said so?'

'Well, he's always giving him the worst jobs, and Mr. Jones says he wouldn't stand for it.'

'What does your da say?'

'Nothing. He just gets on with his work.'

'And a good job, too. Does Mr. Lord say anything?'

'No. But he's not nice to me da, or pleasant, or anything.'

'If I know old Lord, is he ever pleasant? Is he pleasant to the others?'

'No. He's grumpy all the time ... except to me. And he was grumpy with me this morning cos I said "us" instead of "we".'

'Oh my God!' Fanny put her hand to her head. 'The people who go in for fine words! You stick to your guns and don't let them make a lady out of you, or you'll turn into another Mrs. Flannagan and choke yourself.'

'I don't want to be like her,' said Mary Ann with emphasis. 'I won't let them make a lady out of me.'

'That's the ticket. Now go and get washed.'

Mary Ann did as she was told, then had her sup of tea and an inch-thick slice of bread and dripping whilst Fanny cleaned her coat. And when she was ready to go again she stood at the door and smiled up at the old woman. 'Me da always talks about you, Mrs. McBride.'

'Does he now? Well, I hope he says something good.'

'Yes, he does. He says to me ma that he misses your patter.'

Fanny let out a laugh. 'Does he so? Well I miss him an all, tell him. I miss you all more than you know. But go now, else you'll miss that bus again, and it'll be black dark. And tell your ma I'll be over to see her. Goodbye now.'

'Goodbye, Mrs. McBride . . . and ta . . . thanks for me coat and the tea.' Mary Ann ran down the steps. She felt better now; she always felt better after talking with Mrs. McBride, because Mrs. McBride liked her da and she liked people who liked her da.

But once in the street she did not hurry, because she wasn't going to catch the quarter-to-five bus. She was late now and she would likely get wrong in any case, so she would catch the quarter past five, for there were two things she must do – she must pay a visit to the Holy Family and chalk out the writing on the wall. The thought of the Holy Family caused her conscience to move restlessly. She had neglected them for weeks, because there had been nothing to ask them to do, because everything had been nice, but now there would be plenty for them to get on with if things were to remain nice.

With somewhat of the air of a culprit she entered the church and made her way to the side altar. But for a half-moon of candles burning below the altar and the sanctuary lamp, the church was in darkness. But it was not a darkness that could frighten Mary Ann.

She knelt, looking up at the three figures. They looked warm, drawn together in the candlelight; only the Virgin's face was in shadow under her blue hood. After gazing at them for some time, she felt their expressions changing, and her eyes slid down to her joined hands. They looked a bit vexed cos she hadn't been here for months; they looked like her grannie used to look when she went down to Shields to visit her. 'You only come when you're dragged or when you want something,' her grannie would say. But in this present case she had a defence, for she prayed to them in her night prayers, and she looked across the church at them when she was at Mass. But still, it wasn't the same as paying a visit.

She raised her eyes and began, 'I'm sorry, Jesus, Mary and Joseph; I know I should have come afore, after all you did for us . . . getting me da the job and us the cottage, and putting our Michael to the grammar school, and making me

22

ma happy. But I've been so full up with things. And it gets dark at nights and I've got to catch the half-past-four bus else me ma worries.'

This thought stopped her colloquy . . . Eeh! Her ma would be worrying now. Well, it was no use, it was done. She had missed the quarter-to-five . . . She returned to her prayers.

'I've come to tell you, Jesus, Mary and Joseph, what Sarah Flannagan did. She wrote something on the wall about me da. And Lena Ratcliffe saw it, and if she tells her ma and da they might . . .' She stopped again, unable to find words to formulate the vague uneasiness that filled her should the knowledge that her da had drunk heavily ever reach the ears of the farm manager and his wife. She did not reason to herself that Mr. Lord had engaged her father, and that only he could sack him, for she could feel that there were ways and means of bringing about the desired result other than by direct assault . . . subtle, frightening ways.

She began again, 'Well, they might think me da was a bad man, and you know he's not, you know he's the finest da in the world. And he hasn't been . . . sick, even a little bit since we went to the farm. But if Lena tells her ma about him . . .' She paused and glanced down. 'I don't like Lena Ratcliffe. Me ma says I've got to be nice to her, but she's like me grannie and Sarah Flannagan, and I can't. And she's swanky and thinks she's somebody cos her da's the farm boss. And she's jealous of the Lord liking me. Yes, she is.' Her thoughts were loud in her head and the three members of the Holy Family brought their frowns to bear on her.

Eeh! What had she said?

Their censure weighed her down, and her head drooped again and she muttered, 'I'm sorry.' But somehow this did not seem adequate, for they still looked ratty, so she added the confessional formula, 'I'm very sorry I have sinned against thee and by the help of Thy Holy Grace I'll never sin again.' But even this did not soften them; so, self-consciously blessing herself, she stood up, genuflected, then walked up the church and into the blackness.

At the font she blessed herself with the holy water, and stood for a moment thinking: 'And just because I said that . . . Well, she is jealous – I don't care.' It was on this bold and wicked note she went to open the swing door that led into

23

the porch, but as she touched it, it swung in on her, and for the second time that evening she found herself sitting on her bottom. It was as if the Holy Family with one accord had knocked her there.

'In the name of goodness, child, have I hurt you?'

Father Owen picked her up and peered at her. 'Why, it's Mary Ann. Are you hurt?'

'No, Father.'

She didn't sound quite sure.

'What you doing here so late? You should have been home by now.'

'I've been to Mrs. McBride's, and I missed the bus, Father, so I thought I'd pay a visit to the Holy Family.' She hesitated to add what they had done to her through the instrument of himself.

'A very good thought an' all. And now are you all right?' He led her out to the church door, and there, in the light from a street lamp, he looked at her. 'You're a bit white. Did I hurt you now?'

'No, Father . . . no.'

'That's all right then.'

He still continued to stare at her, his hand placed firmly on the top of her hat. 'Is anything wrong, Mary Ann?'

'No, Father.'

He paused awhile. 'Is your da all right?'

'Oh yes . . . yes, Father.'

'He hasn't . . .?'

'No, no, no.' She brought the denial out rapidly. She couldn't bear that the priest should even say the word, even if he should say sick instead of drunk. 'Me da's fine, and so's me ma and our Michael.'

'Well, I'm glad to hear that. . . . Now, you're sure you're all right?'

'Yes, Father.'

'Then off you go. Good night, my child.'

'Good night, Father.'

Mary Ann turned away, but before re-entering the church the priest gazed after her for a moment, and he scratched the sparse grey hair above his ear. He knew Mary Ann, none better, and there was something wrong with her, or else he was a Dutchman. . . .

Mary Ann glanced into Harry Siddon's, the watchmaker. His big clock said five minutes past five. In the light from his window she groped in her school bag and found a piece of chalk. Then she started to run; she'd just have time to scratch the words out before the bus came.

As she turned into Frank Street she saw with relief that there was no one waiting by the stop, so nobody would make any remark when she began to chalk the wall.

The down bus had stopped on the opposite side of the road, and as it moved on a man came hurrying from behind it. He stepped on to the pavement just as she reached the wall.

'Mary Ann!'

So great was the start she gave that the chalk sprang from her hand.

'Where've you been?'

'To . . . to Mrs. McBride's, Da.'

'Why couldn't you tell your mother you were going?'

'I didn't know I was going, Da.'

She could see he was flaming mad, the kind he got when he was worried; he seemed twice as tall and twice as broad. She didn't really mind him being mad at her, she'd rather him be mad at her than at her ma or their Michael, but she was worried nevertheless.

'Lena said you were fighting. Who were you fighting with?'

'Sarah Flannagan.'

'Sarah Flannagan!' he repeated. 'If you don't stop it I'll take the hide off you. D'you hear?'

She made no answer.

'You're like a hooligan.'

They were staring at each her, the father and the daughter, and as a mighty ship can be turned by the slightest touch on the wheel, she turned him to face the road. She did it by holding his eye and moving towards the kerb. Whatever happened he mustn't see what was on the wall. He could be as mad as a hatter with her now but the morrow they'd be all right again. . . . But if he saw what was on the wall . . .

He stood now looking across the road and talking at her. He had his hands in his pockets so that he would not be softened by her touch. She stood a little away from him, her head down, pretending that she was sulking. ... And then she remembered her chalk. It was the only piece she had and she'd dropped it. All the subtlety of her past manoeuvre was lost in turning to retrieve the chalk.

Mike turned and watched her looking on the pavement. He saw her pick up a piece of chalk, and as if it were activated by a malevolent power and wanted to point out to him its purpose, it caused Mary Ann to raise her eyes to the wall. Mike's gaze followed hers, and before she could swing round again to the kerb he had read what was there.

After one glance at his face Mary Ann stared at the road again.

'Give me that chalk.'

Silently she handed him the chalk but she did not look at him as he scrubbed out the words. When the scraping stopped he came to the kerb again and handed her all that was left, a tiny stump. Then he took her hand and held it tightly in his.

When Sarah Flannagan had knocked her into the gutter she hadn't cried; when the priest had knocked her on to her bottom and she'd thought her hip bones were coming through her shoulders she hadn't cried; but now the tears came into her throat and the pain of them choked her and dragged from her a groan. Mike's hands came about her and she was lifted into his arms, and as the bus came she turned her head into his coat so that the people should not see.

CHAPTER TWO

GOING UP IN THE WORLD

'COME on, man, and have a pint. What's a Saturda' afternoon for?' Mr. Jones adjusted his cap and buttoned up his coat. 'What're you going to do with yersel'?'

Mike gave a short laugh. 'I can find plenty to do with meself. I've got that back garden to dig.'

'Oh, to hell, man. Come on, the back garden'll be there when you're not. Look, there's no use in working night and day. What's life for? I'm like yersel', I mean to get on, but I'm not goin' to work me guts out. I'll go up in the world without doing that, ye'll see. Are you comin'?'

'Da, can I weed?'

Mike turned and looked at Mary Ann standing in the doorway. 'Yes, get on with it,' he said, somewhat shortly.

But Mary Ann did not go and get on with it; she stared at Mr. Jones. She had come to a definite decision about Mr. Jones: she didn't like him. He was always egging her da on to do something or other, and she was terrified that repetition would wear Mike down and that one Saturday he would go with Mr. Jones to the village bar.

The four men on the farm had alternate Saturday afternoons off, and every other Saturday, when Mike and he were off together, Mr. Jones would repeat his invitation. He liked Mike. He considered him a man's man, but he couldn't understand why he was sticking so hard to the water wagon. He guessed that it was his wife who was at the bottom of it. She was a bit high-hat, at least his missus thought so. But then Clara thought everyone high-hat who was different from herself. She had to remember, as he was continually pointing out to her, that they were lucky to have the Shaughnessys as neighbours, for they didn't grumble about having their rightful half of the yard.

The yard behind the cottages had once been part of a second stable-yard, and no dividing fence separated the cottages. The two back doors and the kitchen and bedroom windows all faced the yard. Except for a rain barrel, a lean-to and a stack of logs the Shaughnessys' side was clear, but on the Joneses' side was a conglomeration of old motor-bikes because Mr. Jones was mechanical-minded.

'Mary Ann!' Lizzie called from the kitchen; and Mary Ann, going hurriedly into the room, said, 'I'm going to weed, Ma.'

'Stay in here a minute.'

'But Ma.'

'Sit down, I say, and leave your da alone.'

27

'But Ma, Mr. Jones . . .' Mary Ann sat down without finishing.

'You needn't worry about Mr. Jones,' said Lizzie.

Screwing uneasily on her chair, Mary Ann watched her mother hanging the cups of the new half set of china she had bought that morning on the hooks of the dresser. She watched her stand back and survey the result. But all the time her irritation was rising, and when there came the clutter of Mike's boots on the stones of the yard, she jumped up, asking eagerly, 'Can I go now, Ma?'

'Yes,' said Lizzie; 'but don't bother him.'

Mary Ann ran out, grabbing a small garden fork from under the lean-to as she went, and she joined Mike as he started to turn over the patch of ground at the side of the cottage.

'Where can I do, Da?'

'Along by the wall there,' he said.

Mary Ann started to dig up the weeds with vigour. She did not chatter, for when her ma said 'Don't bother him' it meant something. It was only four days ago that he had scratched the writing out and he had been funnily quiet since, not boisterous and laughing and throwing her up to the ceiling and carrying on with her ma in the kitchen.

Mrs. Jones, coming out of her front door dressed for town, said, 'Hallo there, Mike. At it again?'

'Aye,' said Mike, 'at it again.'

'You should give yourself a break, man,' said Mrs. Jones, laughing.

Mary Ann watched her go down the path. Mrs. Jones was all right, but she wasn't like Mrs. McBride. She wished Mrs. McBride could live next door. . . . The futility of this wish made her attack the soil with renewed vigour until she became hot with her efforts. She looked at Mike. He didn't look hot, he was digging steadily. She wished he would talk. She had been quiet so long, hours and hours.

The sound of a church clock striking came to her. She didn't know whether the chimes came from Felling or Hebburn, but much to her surprise it struck only two. She'd just have to say something. She straightened her aching back, made a number of coughing sounds, and was just about to lead Mike into conversation when Michael came tearing across the yard.

'Da . . . can I buy some fireworks? Look, Mr. Lord gave it to me.' He held out his palm, with a shilling on it.

'Mr. Lord? Where's he?' Mary Ann dropped her fork and darted to Michael.

'At the farm.'

'You'd better ask your ma,' said Mike. 'I thought you had some for tonight.'

'Only a few.' Michael turned to Mary Ann. 'He gave Lena a shilling an' all.'

Mary Ann stared at her brother, then with an exaggerated show of indifference she said, 'I don't care.'

'Do you know what, Da? Mr. Lord's going to build a house here.'

Mike straightened up. 'Who told you that?'

'I heard him and Mr. Ratcliffe talking. I wasn't meaning to listen or anything.' Michael cast a scathing glance at his sister which dissociated him from any connection with her tactics of getting information. 'He was talking over in the yard. The architect's coming on Monday.'

Mike, pulling a face, raised his eyebrows and pursed his lips, but he made no comment; but Mary Ann's comments came tumbling over each other. 'Build a house here! Oh, goody. He'll take us to school every morning and I'll be able to go in the house every day and . . . and he won't be lonely, and he'll likely get rid of old Ben, cos you couldn't have him in the new house, and he'll get a young servant who won't be so bossy.'

Michael sniffed disdainfully and went into the house. Within a few minutes Mary Ann watched him come out again and run across the yard and along the narrow lane which led to the village.

'I bet me ma's let him spend it, and she wouldn't me.' On this thought, she too sped into the house, crying, 'Ma, have you let our Michael buy fireworks?'

'Yes,' said Lizzie. 'And go and tell your da there's a cup of tea ready.'

'Aw . . . w, you wouldn't let me. Can I spend me da's sixpence?'

Lizzie sighed. 'You've got fireworks for tonight.'

'Only a few, Ma. And now our Michael and Lena'll have piles.'

'Oh, go on then,' said Lizzie; 'there'll be no peace until you do. But mind, don't start moaning at Christmas because there's nothing in your box.'

Christmas was as a thousand light-years away from the fifth of November; in fact it might never come at all. She dashed to her school purse which was hanging on a long strap at the back of the cupboard door, extracted a solitary six-pence and dashed out of the house. She had reached the lane before she remembered the tea, and from there she shouted, 'There's some tea for you, Da,' then ran like the wind in case their Michael and Lena Ratcliffe should buy up the shop.

Wilson's stores, standing between the Boar's Head and a row of grey stone cottages and dead opposite the Methodist chapel, sold everything but beer, coke and coal. Inside the shop, in the small space left for customers, stood Michael and Lena. They had already made their purchases and seemed to have acquired a considerable amount for their money, but, Mary Ann noticed scornfully, they were all little 'uns that wouldn't make very big bangs, so, just to show them, she decided to spend the entire sixpence at one go.

'I want a One o'Clock Gun, please,' she said.

Swiftly Michael turned on her. 'You're not to buy One o'Clock Guns, me ma said so.'

'She didn't so,' said Mary Ann. And this was true, for Lizzie had not forbidden her to buy such a firework, never dreaming that she would attempt to do so, knowing that she was afraid of big bangs.

'You'll get into trouble,' said Michael.

She hesitated. Yes, that was true, she likely would. She was still hesitating when Lena said. 'We've got two One o'Clock Guns for tonight.'

That did it. Had Mary Ann suspected that secreted within the firework was a time bomb she would still have bought it.

'Now, do you want it or not?' asked Mrs. Wilson.

'Yes, please.'

Michael walked out of the shop and Lena followed, and when Mary Ann joined them, with a fat red stick of gunpowder in her hand, Michael said, 'You won't half catch it if me ma finds you with that, you'll see.'

'Tell-tale, long tongue!' said Mary Ann.

'Come on,' said Lena.

'Where're you going?' asked Mary Ann.

'To our hut.'

'Can I come?'

'No,' said Lena.

Mary Ann watched Michael. It was his turn to hesitate. He half turned to her, but finally succumbed to Lena's delicate manoeuvre of pulling him forcibly by the arm.

'Spoonies!' cried Mary Ann after them. 'Sloppy doppies!'

She had the satisfaction of seeing Michael bounce round and make for her. She did not, however, wait for his coming, but scampered away in the opposite direction, homewards. Once in the lane, her running turned into a slow walk, for ahead of her was Mr. Jones, and he wasn't walking quite straight but with his usual Saturday-afternoon gait. She let him enter his cottage before she crossed the yard. She was no longer carrying the One o'Clock Gun in her hand, for she knew quite well that she would lose it if her ma saw it. There were some matches kept just inside the scullery door. She proposed to pinch a few, then light the firework and throw it as far away from her as possible.

The kitchen door was closed, and the sound of voices came from behind it, but so intent was Mary Ann on securing the matches that for once her curiosity was not to the fore. The matches safely tucked under the elastic of her bloomers, and trembling at her daring, she made her way into the lane again and stood silently considering where would be the best place to let it off. The bottom field where the cows were would do. This decision spurred her to climb three gates – she preferred the arduous climb to shutting the gates after her – and to make her way round the edges of two ploughed fields. After all this labour she reached the selected field only to decide against it. The placidity of the cows at their munching stayed her hand, for it brought back their teacher's warning to all the class not to set fireworks off when there were any animals about.

Slowly now, and rather dismally, she wandered back to the lane. The only thing for it was to set it off here. It wouldn't be much fun, but she could see no other safe place.

She struck a match, but before it got within an inch of the fuse she dropped it. Refusing to admit her fear, she lit another. This she only allowed to singe the end of the fuse before dropping that, too. She was busy with the fourth attempt when she heard coming from the main road, which was screened from her by the bank and the hedge, the sound of Lena's voice, and a great idea sprang into her head. It lifted her feet off the ground and sent her flying along the lane. She'd set it off and give them the shock of their lives. Reaching the yard, she darted in a zig-zag fashion through Mr. Jones's jumble of bikes and entered his lean-to, which was about three feet from the cottage bedroom window, and there crouched down.

As once again she fumbled with the matches the sound of deep snores came to her, and glancing to her left she saw between the curtains and through the partly open window the prostrate figure of Mr. Jones fast asleep in bed. His mouth was open and he was anything but a pleasant sight. He looked awful, Mary Ann thought.

The match struck, she applied it with a steadier hand now that she had a definite purpose. When they crossed the yard she'd throw it behind them, not too near, but near enough to make them jump out of their skins, cos her ma had said if you must throw squibs never throw them in anybody's face, it might blind them. Her whole body was shaking with excitement. The fuse was nearly alight, and there was Lena and their Michael just entering the yard. Her heart pumping rapidly, she was holding the sizzling stick out ready to throw, when a terrible thing happened. From out of her own doorway stepped Mr. Lord and her da.

Her mind, usually as nimble as mercury, refused to suggest what she should do now. Her main feeling at the moment was that Mr. Lord had been in their house and she hadn't known – she had missed something. Then her mind swung back to the job in hand and she became petrified ... if she threw the One o'Clock Gun it would explode right between her da and Mr. Lord and Lena and their Michael.

Mr. Lord hated fireworks – he had said so only yesterday. Now her agile brain was working at such a speed that the flame, travelling along the fuse, seemed to become stationary. She must do something with the thing. It had ceased to be a One o'Clock Gun or even a firework, it had become a Thing – an awful Thing. Throw it near Mr. Lord she couldn't. The only alternative was to let it go off here ... and die. Eeh! but she couldn't do that either, she was scared of big bangs. Eeh ... Hail Mary, full of Grace ... Mary Ann felt she had been holding the firework at least a week instead of a few seconds, and the fuse, racing now with her thoughts, was getting shorter at a speed that both fascinated and terrified her and almost robbed her of the power to fling the Thing anywhere at all. Then, seemingly of its own volition, the firework sprang from her hand and flew through the open window and right under Mr. Jones's bed.

The sound of the explosion, hemmed in as it was by the cottage walls, had differing effects on those who heard it. It caused Mr. Lord to jump as if the firework had been tied to his coat tails, and Mike to start and gaze in perplexity towards his neighbour's door. It acted on both Michael and Lena in the same way. It sprang open their eyes and mouths to their widest, for instantly they both knew what had caused the bang and who had caused it, and their astonishment made them look senseless. But the effect on Mary Ann was to lift her off her feet and precipitate her into the middle of the spare parts, where she lay covering her head with her hands to stop the cottage from falling on her.

What effect her sudden appearance had on the four people in the yard was lost in that of a greater surprise, for following on an unearthly wail the cottage door was pulled open and there raced into the yard the apparition of Mr. Jones.

Clad only in his shirt and linings, and making almost animal sounds, Mr. Jones had the appearance of a madman intent on winning a marathon, and it took all Mike's strength, which was considerable, to bring the little man to a halt and to hold him.

'Steady, man, steady!' cried Mike.

Mr. Jones, panting as if at the end of a race, and his face

working in much the same way as that of a straining and spent runner, gasped, 'In the n . . . name of G . . . God, Mike. . . .'

'Steady, man!' said Mike again.

'B-but, Mike . . .'

Mary Ann rose from her knees with all eyes upon her, including Lizzie's. Mr. Jones, still jangling, was holding on to Mike as he stared at the perpetrator of the crime. No one spoke as she moved forward. Mr. Lord's face was very red and her da's unusually white. That was temper, Mary Ann knew. Michael and Lena looked as if they had been struck dead.

Lizzie's voice was low as she said, 'Get inside.'

Mary Ann got inside. She was so frightened she thought she was going to vomit. She sat on the kitchen chair with her legs tightly crossed and waited. After a while Lena came to the open door and looked at her as if she were some strange specimen in a cage, then she walked away again without saying a word.

Mary Ann sat for a long while. She heard voices and movement in the cottage next door. Then there was quiet for a moment before they all came back into the kitchen: her ma and da, their Michael and Mr. Lord. And when she looked at her da she wanted to leave the room, so affected was she by the anger she saw in his face.

Then before her da could say a word Mr. Lord suddenly sat down, his red face turned to purple as if he, too, were on the verge of exploding. And then he did, but not with the sudden impact of the firework. First the muscles of his face worked, then his body shook and he groaned and put his hand to his side, then he strained back in his chair and said, 'Oh dear! oh dear! . . . the funniest sight . . . the funniest sight.' As the tears began to rain down his cheeks the tension in the room slackened somewhat. Mary Ann, with one eye on Mike, gave the semblance of a watery smile; Lizzie and Michael seemed to breathe more freely; only Mike remained the same. He was apparently unaffected by Mr. Lord's laughter, and glared at Mary Ann.

'Why did you do it?' he demanded.

'I didn't mean to, Da.'

'Then why?'

34

Mary Ann made no answer, and Mike's voice, rising, demanded again, 'Why?'

Trembling now, Mary Ann said, 'Cos I was frightened of it going off near me, and if I'd thrown it at Michael and Lena it would have frightened—' Her eyes slid to where Mr. Lord sat dabbing at his eyes.

'Why did you throw it at all? I've warned you about big crackers, haven't I?'

Mary Ann didn't stress the fine point here that it was Michael he had warned, but with her eyes stretched wide she continued to stare at him. Even when Mr. Lord said, 'Don't worry, don't worry. He wanted stirring up anyway, that fellow,' she still continued to gaze at her da.

'It might have turned the man's mind.' Mike spoke down to the top of Mr. Lord's head and there was not the slightest deference in his voice.

And now Mary Ann looked a little fearfully from Mike to Mr. Lord, but Mr. Lord still seemed amused and he said, 'What, a bang like that, and the fellow been through the war?'

'That's a different thing,' said Mike, 'you're expecting bangs then.'

'He shouldn't have been in bed on a Saturday afternoon. And he was likely half drunk,' said Mr. Lord, tersely.

Was it her imagination or was there a sort of warning in Mr. Lord's voice? But it was no imagination that her da stiffened, and the stiffness came over in his tone: 'It was the man's own time.'

'Yes, yes, his own time.' Mr. Lord stood up abruptly, and Lizzie, looking fearfully from one to the other, asked: 'Won't you stay and have a cup of tea, sir?'

'No, no, thank you,' he said, and much to her amazement he smiled kindly at her. 'I've had all the beverage I want for one afternoon.' His hand went out and he rumpled Mary Ann's hair, and Mike, seeming to become more hostile and addressing Mary Ann pointedly, said: 'You're not getting off with this this time, you're in for a good smacked backside, and don't you forget it.'

'Nothing of the kind.' The old man swung round on Mike. 'You're treating the thing too seriously.'

'I know me own business, sir, if you don't mind.'

Now they were facing each other, hostility in their eyes.

Lizzie's hand went to her throat. She prayed that Mike might keep his temper. Oh, were things never to run smoothly? She knew that Mike's nerves were on edge – the desire for a drink had been in him for days. He had been coping, and had himself well in hand, until last Tuesday and the incident of the writing on the wall. Things like that affected him. 'I might as well just be at it again,' he had said. 'They're waiting for me to start . . . I can feel it.' And she had cried back at him, 'Nonsense! The doings of a girl like Sarah Flannagan. And you know her mother, she hasn't a good word for God.' And on top of all this Mr. Jones had to come in today when he was well under way and jabber and jabber. It was all telling on Mike. If only Mr. Lord would go and she could talk to him.

Mr. Lord turned from Mike and moved to the door, and there he turned again and said, 'Don't thrash her.' And although he said it quietly, it was an order.

Now anger rose in Lizzie against her daughter. Mike had been made to appear as if thrashing Mary Ann was a pastime of his, when the truth was he had never raised a hand to her in his life . . . he had spoilt her. He may, for a time, have made her own life a hell, but never intentionally Mary Ann's. Even before Mr. Lord was out of earshot, she cried to Mary Ann, 'Get up those stairs and into bed.'

Without a word, and at the double, Mary Ann went.

'And you too!' cried Lizzie to Michael.

'But, Ma, I've done nothing . . . and I'll not go up with her.'

'Then go on out.'

Michael went out, his face expressing the injustice of the dismissal.

Lizzie looked to where Mike was standing staring into the fire, his hands thrust into his pockets, and said softly, 'Take no heed.'

He swung round on her. 'Take no heed! He acts as if he owns me, body and soul. And not only me . . . he gave me the job because of her, and he's taken her.'

'Don't be silly.' Lizzie moved to him, and placing her hands beneath his loose cardigan she gripped his braces and pulled him to her. 'Nobody can take her from you.'

'No? Why is he going to build his house here?'

'Oh!' She leant back from him. 'Mike, that's madness. He's fond of her, I know, but he's got no need to build a house here to see her. He can come in the car as often as he likes. . . . Oh, that's a silly idea, if ever there was one.'

'I don't know so much.'

'It is. You know what he said. He's retiring from an active part in his yard, and now feels he must have something to fill his time. It's only reasonable he wants to build a house on his own land and be near his farm.'

'Why did he have to come and explain it to us? It's none of our business, is it? I'm only a hand here.'

'He's lonely,' said Elizabeth. 'Can't you see? For all his money he's lonely, and he doesn't get on with people – he's kept away from them too long.'

'All I can see is he wants to run her life and mine. Well, I'll give him a good working day, but from then on me life's me own . . . and hers is mine an' all, until she can look after herself.'

He jerked himself from her hands and, taking up his cap, went out, whilst Lizzie, after staring at the closed door for a moment, braced herself before going up the stairs.

Mary Ann was sitting on the side of the bed, her eyes fixed wide in her drawn face.

'You see what you've done? You've got your da into trouble with Mr. Lord. Are you satisfied?'

Mary Ann's face became even whiter, and her eyelids drooped as if she were about to faint. Her silence was more telling than any verbal defence.

The tenseness went out of Lizzie's body, and moving her head in bewilderment she went to the bed and, sitting down, slowly drew her daughter into her arms.

Like a small avalanche Mary Ann's pent-up emotion was released. Sobbing and crying, she clung to her mother, while Lizzie rocked her, saying, 'There now, there now, it's all over. It's all right, it's all right. Stop that crying, it's all right.' But as she was saying it she wondered in her own mind whether it was all right. Mary Ann would forget most of the happenings of today; only the funny parts would remain, and tomorrow the whole family would likely be laughing at the recollection of Mr. Jones tearing from the house. Yes ... even Mike, for it bore out Mr. Jones's oft-used prophecy that he would rise in the world. But would the deep implications that the event had brought to the surface be forgotten? There had always seemed to be a state of undeclared war existing between Mike and Mr. Lord, but this incident had brought about an open declaration. There could be only one victor in such a war – Mike. And what would the victory entail?

Suddenly Lizzie felt very weary.

CHAPTER THREE

CHRISTMAS

THE kitchen was rich with the smells of cooking. There was the pastry smell, a mince smell, a herb smell, the smell of boiling bacon, and the warm sweet smell of cocoa.

Mary Ann let the steam from her mug waft about her face; then she stuck her tongue down into the froth on the surface of the cocoa and licked at it.

'Don't do that!' said Lizzie, turning from the baking board.

'Well, it's hot, Ma. Ma ...'

'Yes?'

'Lena says that Mr. Lord's goin' t'give her a great big present.'

'That's nice.'

'Do you think he will?'

'Lena must think so, else she wouldn't have said so.'

'I think she's a liar.'

'Don't use that word!'

'Well,' Mary Ann took a sip of her cocoa, 'Sarah Flannagan calls me that, and' – she glanced covertly at Lizzie – 'others do an' all.'

Lizzie suppressed her smile while redoubling her efforts with the rolling-pin.

'Look, there's me da.' Mary Ann jumped from her chair and made for the window, spilling her cocoa as she did so. And Lizzie cried, 'Look what you're doing!'

She, too, looked through the window across the yard to where Mike was striding towards the cottage. It was eleven o'clock in the morning, and not the usual time for him to come in; he had his break at ten. But his brows weren't drawn, and he looked cheery . . . and handsome, she thought, like he did when they were first married. The winter sun was shining on his mop of red hair and lightening still further the new clearness of his skin. He was looking ten years younger than he did when they lived in Jarrow. But what was bring-ing him here at this time?

'Da, d'you want some cocoa?' asked Mary Ann.

'Yes. And anything else that's going . . . something smells good.' He came and stood near Lizzie, and dipping his finger into the flour he rubbed it on to her cheek.

Mary Ann gurgled. It always gave her a feeling of joy to see her ma and da larking on.

'Give over.' Lizzie pushed him with her elbow. 'What are you here for, anyway?'

Mike, hitching up his trousers, said with slow, exaggerated airiness, 'His lordship's asked me to accompany him into Newcastle. Me, Mike Shaughnessy, as ever was.'

'Mr. Lord?'

'Mr. Lord . . . his honour . . . his worship.'

'Oh, Da, can I come?'

'You cannot. . . . Bejapers! Not even a queen would I allow to accompany me the day.'

Mike was amused, he was happy; and although he scoffed and put on the Irish twang, Lizzie could see he was pleased.

'What are you going in for?' she asked.

'I haven't a notion, me darlin'.'

Mary Ann laughed out loud, and Mike, looking at Lizzie, made a tiny movement with his eyes towards her. And after a pause Lizzie said, 'It's time you were going to meet your grannie. Go on, get your coat on.'

Mary Ann's face suddenly fell. She knew she was being got rid of. 'Aw! . . . it's ten minutes afore the bus comes; and it'd freeze you out.'

'Get your coat on,' said Lizzie callously, 'and freeze. You

haven't frozen, I notice, during the last two hours you've been out. . . . And mind,' she warned her daughter, 'of what I told you last night.'

Mary Ann got into her coat, hat, scarf and gloves at a snail's pace, and saying to anyone it might concern, 'I never get taken nowhere,' she went out.

Mike and Lizzie looked at each other and smiled.

'Why is he taking you?' asked Lizzie.

'I'm not exactly sure,' said Mike, 'but I think it's to buy me Lady Jane something.' He nodded in the direction of the window, through which Mary Ann could be seen slowly crossing the yard. 'But I know this much,' he added, 'I'll have to pay for me jaunt. Ratcliffe's furious; in fact, he tried to stop me going. He told him I was needed to load beet, and the old boy said why not put one of the others outside, it'd do them good. He keeps his eyes open, I'll grant him that. But Ratcliffe'll swear I've been mewing to him.'

'Let him swear what he likes,' said Lizzie. She was happy to think Mr. Lord held no feeling of animosity towards Mike, for she had been worried sick since the firework episode. 'Do you think someone's told him about Ratcliffe giving you all the tough jobs?' she asked.

'Not on your life. Which of them would concern himself about me?' said Mike scornfully. 'Jonesy might tell me what to say, but he'd never say it for me. And Stan and Joe are for ever sucking up to Ratcliffe. . . . No, the old fellow's not blind. He engaged me as cowman afore Ratcliffe came, and what does he see when he comes around. . . . I'm anywhere but in the byres.'

'Then why doesn't he say something to Ratcliffe?'

'Well, I suppose fair's fair. You put a man in as manager, you've got to let him manage.'

Lizzie, turning to the board, cut a spray of leaves from out of the pastry and placed them on top of a pie. Then she said quietly, 'I don't like him, Mike . . . I don't trust him. Nor her. I'd be careful if I was you.'

He came close to her side again, but did not immediately answer her. Instead he stood looking at the gold coils of her hair lying low down on her neck, and his finger traced the curve of the twined braids before he said softly, 'Don't you worry, I know what's at stake. It'll take more than Ratcliffe to get me on the wrong foot. The old fellow can do it more easily than him.'

'Oh Mike, be careful.' Lizzie turned her face to his and her eyes added a plea to her voice. 'Don't say anything to him you'll be sorry for. Don't, Mike.'

'Now look,' he pulled her round, gathering her floured hands into his great fists. 'Haven't I behaved meself and kept me tongue quiet . . . and haven't I done what I said about the other business? I've never touched a drop. And it hasn't been easy, mind.'

'Oh Mike, I know, I know. Only I get frightened.'

'Well, don't.'

She leant her face towards him and rested her cheek against his. His lips touched her ear, and she stayed still for a moment. Then, suddenly pulling herself from him, she exclaimed in indignant tones, 'Eleven o'clock on a Saturday morning and tomorrow Christmas Eve! And I suppose Mr. Lord's waiting patiently for you?' Her face was flushed, and her eyes happy and he brought his hand with a resounding whack upon her buttocks, saying, 'Big Liz.'

'Oh Mike, that hurts!' She held the affected parts.

'You asked for it,' said Mike, putting on his cap. 'Turning a man's head. I'm off now and I don't know what time I'll be back . . . that's if I come back at all. If I should see a nice little piece in Newcastle, something on the lines of Nellie Flannagan . . .'

He was gone, leaving Lizzie laughing and happy. But still in the midst of it she turned her eyes to the corner of the room where hung a passe-partout framed picture of the Virgin, the work of Mary Ann, and voicelessly she prayed, 'Let it last.'

Mary Ann stood at the crossroads, the wind chafing the only exposed part of her, which was her face. She did not turn her back to it but faced it squarely and told herself she would freeze to death and it would serve them right. There followed in her mind a distinct picture of her death-bed scene. She was lying in bed dressed all in white. Her ma was begging her not to die, her da was crying like anything and so was their Michael, and Father Owen was there, and Mr. Lord and Mrs. McBride . . . and Lena Ratcliffe and Sarah

Flannagan. She had, with the beneficence always attached to the dying, sent for these two to bestow on them her forgiveness. She had reached the scene where she was telling Sarah, in a very weak voice of course, that if she would swear that she had never heard her, Mary Ann, tell a lie in her life she'd speak to the Holy Family for her when she got up to Heaven, when the loud honk-honk of a motor horn made her swing round, and there was her da and Mr. Lord waving. Frantically she waved back, but she doubted if they saw her, or if they cared for that matter. Fancy them not stopping. This affront wiped out even her mother's callousness. And yet as the car disappeared into the distance the wonder of what she had just witnessed dawned on her. ... Mr. Lord was taking her da to Newcastle. Mr. Lord must like her da very much. Suddenly her body became alive with activity. She jumped, she skipped, she took giant strides along the grass verge to a field gate and back again. She flung her arms about the sign-post and endeavoured to climb it. After numerous failures she was half-way up it when the bus stopped on the other side of the road and her grannie alighted.

Mary Ann, lost in her present joy and forgetting why she was at the cross-roads at all, did not see Mrs. McMullen trotting across the road. She was not aware of her presence until she spoke.

'You get your clothes cheap.'

Mary Ann, gripping the pole, was now on eye level with her grannie, and that small, dark, energetic lady, who carried her sixty-seven years with a lightness that chilled the hope of those who relied upon years alone to carry her off, drew in her mouth before opening it to command, 'Get down out of that! Are you stuck there for life?'

Mary Ann's convulsive grasp on the pole slackened, and she sped the short distance to the ground so quickly that she lost her balance and fell down in a heap on to the road.

'That's right,' cried Mrs. McMullen, 'roll in the mud! You get worse. You were bad enough afore. Look at the sight of you.'

Mary Ann did not follow her grannie's pointing finger and look at her coat. She continued to stare glumly at her grannie, and some private section of her mind, kept solely to deal with her hated relative and kept closed these past months, opened and addressed itself to whoever was responsible for her grannie's presence on this globe at all. Why had you to go and let her come, it said, after I asked you to keep her away? You could've done something to her, given her rheumatics or something. But, she ended with truth, nothing ever happens to me grannie.

'Well, come on. Are you going to stand here and freeze us? How far is it? Why didn't your mother come?'

'It's not far, just along the road and down the lane. Me ma's baking.'

They walked away with at least four feet separating them, Mrs. McMullen looking about her with critical eyes. Bare trees, wet brown fields and not a house to be seen; you couldn't even see the top of the gantries in the shipyards only a couple of miles away. Her eyes fell or seemed to be dragged down to her grand-daughter, and she noticed with disapproval that there was colour in her cheeks. But it wouldn't last long, she comforted herself. The child was small and puny by nature and she wouldn't be surprised if there wasn't T.B. there somewhere, brought over from the Shaughnessy family. Even her embittered mind could not actually pin the consumption on the great brawny Mike.

'It's a God-forsaken place you've come to. Your ma didn't get out much afore, she'll get out less here.'

'She does get out. Me da takes her on a Saturda' night, and us an' all, me and our Michael. We go to the pictures. Sometimes we go to Newcastle.'

Mrs. McMullen's eyes and head jerked upwards, and her hat, perched high on top of her abundant hair, looked in danger of toppling off. 'Another brilliant start,' she said, backing up her words with a significant cough.

Mary Ann's eyes, screwed up like gimlets, fixed themselves on her grannie's profile. She was starting again. Why had she to come, anyway? No one had asked her. She had written asking to come, and her ma had said last night, 'Well, she's got to come sometime. And it's Christmas; we must bury the hatchet.'

Mary Ann wished with swift urgency that somebody would spring out of the hedge and hit her grannie with a hatchet ... and run away again, for she wouldn't want anyone to get wrong for hitting her grannie.

'What's the people like?'

'Who ... who d'you mean?'

'The farm men and the manager, of course.' Mrs. McMullen looked at her grand-daughter as if she was a halfwit, for Mary Ann was weighing her answer. If she were to say what she thought, it would be, 'Mr. Ratcliffe's awful, and Mrs. Ratcliffe's snooty, like Lena, and I don't like Mr. Jones, but Stan and Joe are all right,' but being wise to the fact that her grannie would immediately take sides with those she disliked and connect the reason for her dislike with her da, she said, 'They're all right.'

'That's a change.'

This caustic remark demanded no reply, and in silence they continued down the lane. The silence was enforced on the old woman for she had to keep her feet clear of the potholes. But at last she exclaimed, 'Never seen anything like it ... you could break your neck on a dark night.'

Maybe this statement gave rise to the hope in her mind that this would happen to her son-in-law, for she followed it immediately with, 'How often has your da been drunk since he's been here?'

Mary Ann stopped dead and watched her grannie step over a puddle near the grass verge. She had an almost overwhelming desire to take a running jump at the old woman and push her into the ditch.

The word 'drunk' when connected with her da always had the power to make her feel sick. The word was a weapon so powerful that it overshadowed not only her own life but also that of the entire family. What it had almost done in the past it could do again. It had almost parted her ma and da and it had made their Michael gas himself. And there was the other thing it had nearly done, vague in her mind now but still recognized as a bad thing, and made more bad still because her grannie came into it. In fact her grannie seemed to be the master of this particular evil. Her grannie could do again what she had done at Mulhattan's Hall, talk and talk to her ma in the scullery about her da drinking, then end up by mentioning Mr. Quinton and his fine car – she always ended up with Mr. Quinton.

'What you looking like that for? Don't you start any of your tantrums afore I get me foot inside the door. And answer me question.'

'Me da doesn't drink, he's a grand—'

'Yes, yes, I know. He's a grand man, and for God's sake don't start that again.'

'Well, he is.'

'All right, have it your own way. And don't you bawl at me or I'll take the side of your ear off you.'

'I'm not bawling ... me da doesn't drink. He doesn't even go in the village bar, so there. He's fine and respected and everybody likes him. Mr. Lord's taken him in his own car right into Newcastle, and he was sitting aside Mr. Lord and . . .'

'Oh my God! that's enough.' Mrs. McMullen flapped her hand in the air. 'He'll be the Archangel Gabriel next and covered with down. How much further have we got to go along this God-forsaken road?'

Mary Ann gave her no answer, but her indignation carried her some distance ahead of the old woman until they reached the gate, then she ran up the path and round to the back and into the kitchen.

'Where's your grannie?' Lizzie turned from the oven.

Mary Ann tore off her hat. 'She's comin'.'

Lizzie, looking keenly at her daughter, said, 'Now mind, I'm having no trouble. Keep that tongue of yours quiet.'

'She's—'

'That's enough. Where did you leave her?'

'At the gate.'

A hammering on the front door told Lizzie that her mother was no longer at the gate. Forcing a smile to her lips and stiffening her shoulders as if she were going into battle, she went to open the door, saying over her shoulder, 'You stay out to play. Go over to the byres, it's warm there.'

The afternoon had passed off not unpleasantly. Mrs. McMullen had shown no approval of anything in the cottage, but still she had not voiced her disapproval, except about the condition of the road and the distance from the bus. This latter grouse had not been displeasing to Lizzie, for

45

she thought that it would hasten her mother's departure before Mike should come in. Although he knew of his mother-in-law's proposed visit, there had been no mention of it between them, and as he had not returned to dinner she hoped now that he would not return before tea-time. He had not forbidden Mrs. McMullen the house, yet Lizzie knew he would hate to see her in it. Perhaps he was already back on the farm and was not going to put in an appearance until she was gone.

When it was half-past three, however, and Mrs. McMullen was showing no signs of taking her leave, Lizzie became uneasy. And not about this alone. She knew from experience that if into her mother's small talk there should creep a note of mystery, it brooked no good. Three times already during the afternoon her mother had alluded to a surprise that was in store for her, and now she was at it again. Sipping at her seventh cup of tea since her arrival, she was saying, musingly, 'Funny how things turn out. . . . By! it is. But you'll get a surprise one of these days . . . you will that. I've told you, I know more than you think.'

'Look, Mother' – Lizzie endeavoured to keep her impatience from being revealed in her voice – 'don't be so mysterious. What can surprise me? I think I've had all the surprises I want in my life. If this is something unpleasant, let me know now.'

'Who said it was unpleasant?'

Mrs. McMullen put her cup down carefully into the saucer and surveyed it, first from one angle, then from another, before continuing, 'It might be for some. It all depends how you look at it, and who looks at it, and what you look at.'

Lizzie went into the scullery. She could not trust her tongue. It might be for some. She knew what that portended – trouble with or for Mike. Why was her mother so vindictive? Why did she continue to hate him?

'Aren't you going to put a light on, I can hardly see a finger afore me?'

In answer to the querulous demand, Lizzie returned to the kitchen and switched on the light, saying, 'Yes, it's dark sooner than ever tonight.' Then she added, 'You're going to find it difficult getting to the bus.'

46

'I got here, didn't I? Well, I'll get back. Don't worry about me. Where's that 'un? Running the roads, and it near dark.'

'She'll likely be somewhere on the farm. There's no worry about her being out in the dark here.'

'No? You'll always have worry with that madam, you mark my words. And Michael, I've only seen him for five minutes. Why couldn't you keep him in? It isn't as if I'm on the doorstep every day.'

'He'll be in the byres ... he likes to help. Will you have another cup of tea?'

'No.'

A silence settled on the room. The glow from the fire, the pink-shaded light reflecting on the Christmas decorations, and the homely furniture gave it an atmosphere of comfort and of gaiety; but it had ceased to charm Lizzie. She knew why her mother was sitting tight. She had no intention of going until she had seen Mike. But why? Even in the past she had always taken her leave before the time Mike was due home.

But any further speculation Lizzie might have made was cut short by Mike's entry – he came in like a strong wind, bursting into the room, seeming to fill it. His presence, like the wind, stirred things with unseen power, although the gay light in his eyes was shadowed on the sight of his mother-in-law. Lizzie felt his excitement, his vitality, his joy at being home again even after only a few hours away from her, and the love in herself answered his. But she kept it veiled from her eyes.

Now Mrs. McMullen rose to her feet. 'I'll have me hat and coat,' she said. She did not look towards Mike, but took her hat from Lizzie and slowly pinned it on her head. Lizzie next helped her into her coat, and as she did so Michael came in, and she said to him, 'Your grannie's just going, are you coming with us to the bus?'

'All right,' said Michael. He did not appear at all eager, and he added, 'But if you want the half past four you'll have to hurry.' Turning from his mother he said to Mike, 'Have you just got back, Da?'

'Just this minute,' said Mike. He spoke pleasantly to the boy while reaching for one of three pipes from a rack to the

47

side of the fireplace. Scraping the bowl, he sat down by the hearth.

Mrs. McMullen paused in her dressing, and her eyes darted from father to son. The friendliness between them was not lost on her, and it both surprised and annoyed her. The boy had never liked Mike, which had been mostly of her doing, and so to think that now Michael could even tolerate his father seemed to her entirely wrong. The wicked should be made to suffer, not only hereafter but now, and they would be. She wasn't done yet, not by a long chalk. She'd have her own back on that big gormless Irishman, if it took the last breath she breathed.

She stood drawing on her gloves, glancing covertly at the back of Mike's head as she did so. Then looking up at her daughter and in a manner which would have led anyone to believe that she was picking up the threads of a conversation just recently dropped, she exclaimed, 'So old skinflint Lord's going to spend his ill-gotten gains and build himself a house here, is he?'

Lizzie stared at her mother. Mr. Lord's name had not been mentioned, nor the building of his house. Her face, screwed up in perplexity, was asking her mother silently how she knew this, when Mrs. McMullen continued, 'It's a small world. Fancy Bob getting that contract. That's a feather in his cap, that. Ten thousand pounds the house will cost afore it's finished. That's some money, isn't it? That's a contract. Well, come on. . . .'

Lizzie stood stiffly watching her mother go from the room. It was almost diabolical the way in which she had manoeuvred this piece of news to hit Mike. This, then, was the surprise.

She could find it in her heart to hate this woman, who was relentless in her attempts to achieve a separation between her and Mike, and all under the guise of wanting nothing but her happiness.

Outwardly Mike had not moved except to draw deeply on his pipe, but the news had caused something to leap within him, a mixture of fear and hate and envy. Slowly he lifted his eyes and looked into the mirror above the mantelpiece. In it he could see Lizzie. Her face was turned from him, and she did not turn towards him or speak a word to him as she followed her mother out. He kept himself still, although some vital part of him had flown through the room and grasped his mother-in-law by the neck and swung her round and away; and he watched her, spinning away and over the hills, over the river, away, away into Eternity, nevermore to touch their lives with her bitterness and venom.

Suddenly he leant forward and sharply knocked his pipe upon the bar, knocking the nodule completely out. So Quinton was coming here to build the old fellow's house. Well, what of it! What of it? Lizzie would see him – she wouldn't be able to help it. His fine car would come into the lane and she would watch him daily directing operations on the hill practically opposite the kitchen window. He would come in here – he was an old friend of hers, he should have been her husband – he would sit in this chair and look at her; and they would laugh together while he was at his work.

As he stood up abruptly the front door banged and Lizzie came into the room. There had not been time for her to go to the crossroads and back again, and Mike looked towards her as she stood within the door pulling off her coat. Neither of them spoke for a moment. Then she said softly, 'Look Mike, I knew nothing about it until a minute ago.'

He stared at her. 'Who's saying anything?'

'But you don't believe me.'

'Who's saying I don't believe you?'

'But I can tell.' She sprang it on me – his name had not been mentioned, or the house, or anything.'

Mike gave a tight laugh. 'Well, now, ask yourself if that doesn't take some believing. The old bitch was full of it. It's hard to imagine her keeping that up her sleeve, and it didn't sound as if she had.'

'But Mike, that's just the point, she had. She did it to cause trouble. She's my mother, and at this moment I hate her.'

So intent was Lizzie in trying to convince Mike of the truth that she took no heed of the click of the outer door. Nor did Mike as he turned from her and looked into the fire and rasped his hands over the dark stubble of his chin before saying, 'She'll never rest till she's done it.'

As Lizzie went to his side and gripped his arm Mary Ann's head came round the door. She had been about to give her

49

da a fright, but her mischievous intent was checked and the impish gleam died out of her eyes as she stared at them. They were fighting, the quiet fighting like they had done in the bedroom at Mulhattan's Hall. Yet they couldn't be fighting, they hadn't had time. Their Michael had just told her that their grannie had gone and their da had just come in.

She saw Lizzie put her arms about Mike and pull him almost fiercely round to her, As she listened to her mother's low, urgent words, the old fear, the fear that at one time had made her want to die, came flooding over her again.

'How often have I told you she can't separate us? Nor can Bob. You're the only one that can do that. Haven't I told you, Mike? Let him come and build the house, what does it matter? I don't want a car or a fine house; I only want you and what you can give me. Do you believe me? Mike, tell me. . . .'

Mary Ann watched her da look into her mother's eyes with that lost look she knew so well; then with a suddenness that drove the breath from Lizzie's body he pulled her into his arms.

The fact that they were kind again was no solace to Mary Ann. Quietly she retreated, her gloved fingers pushed deep into her mouth. It was her grannie had done it. She had made Mr. Quinton come and build the house for Mr. Lord and upset her da. . . . Oh, her grannie! If only she would drop down dead.

She stood under the lean-to biting on her fingers for some time. She stood until she felt the cold creep up past her knees, and one foot went dead. But what did it matter? All of a sudden everything was spoiled, Christmas and Mr. Lord's house, even the reason for the visit to Newcastle.

With flooding eyes she stared upwards into the sky. Venus was making its way towards its zenith. Tomorrow night that big star, she knew, would come to rest over the stable, and Jesus would be born. And as she stared, she was not surprised to see the star wink at her. It grew brighter and bigger every time she blinked her tears away, and brighter and bigger still, until right in the centre she actually saw the Infant Himself.

Her hands under her arm-pits, she swayed now backwards and forwards trying to still the cold, and as she swayed the

Child nodded to her. 'Go on in,' He said. 'Go on in now and be nice to your da. And the morrow pay a visit to the Crib and we'll see what can be done.'

After she had blown her nose, the star decreased to its normal size, and slowly she went indoors.

Her da was sitting before the fire as if nothing had happened, and her ma turned and smiled at her. She took off her hat and coat and went and stood between her da's knees and pressed herself close to him.

'You're cold,' he said. 'Are you all right?'

'Yes,' she answered.

'Don't you want to ask me anything about Newcastle?'

She shook her head.

Mike lifted his eyes to Lizzie and she came and, bending over Mary Ann, asked, 'Do you feel bad?'

'No.'

'Have you been fighting?'

'No.'

'Put your tongue out then.'

Mary Ann stuck out her tongue to its surprising length, and Lizzie said, 'Well, just in case you'll have a dose of syrup of figs, and off to bed with you.'

When there was no objection to this, Lizzie and Mike looked at each other with knowledge in their eyes. They knew the reason for their daughter's quietness. As usual, with or without intention, she had been listening.

Lizzie turned away, and Mike bent his head and rubbed his face reassuringly against his daughter's cheek.

CHAPTER FOUR

THE OLD FIRM

LIZZIE lifted the square box on to the bus platform and said to the conductor, 'Will you help her off with it at Pratt's Lane, please?' But before that obliging man could agree,

Mary Ann exclaimed for the twenty-sixth time that morning, 'I tell you I can carry it meself!'

Lizzie stepped back, not so much to avoid being knocked over as to restrain herself from lifting Mary Ann off the bus and boxing her ears.

As the bus began to move, Mary Ann looked from her mother's set face to Michael, who was standing by her side, and, as was her way, she was suddenly overcome with remorse – it was because of her persistence and tantrums that Michael wasn't coming with her to give Mr. Lord the cake. Gripping the rail, she leant forward and shouted, 'You can take me own Christmas box to him by yourself this afternoon, you can.'

But Michael's reaction to this offer was lost on her, for the conductor, holding her securely by the collar, pushed her into the bus and on to a seat. He placed the box by her side, saying, 'You're going to have your work cut out carrying that, it's nearly as big as you. Is anybody meeting you?'

'No – and I can carry it.'

'Well, if you say you can, you can.'

Left to her own thoughts Mary Ann looked at the box, and her eye penetrated the wrapping and saw lying snugly in layers of soft paper the Christmas cake, all iced and beautiful. She gave a deep sigh; she was taking it on her own to him. And she was surprised that she was, for it was only just before going to sleep last night that she had decided she must take the cake to Mr. Lord all by herself, because if their Michael went with her as arranged it would be impossible for her to talk to Mr. Lord, and it was absolutely necessary now, after what she had heard, that she should do so. The new threat to her parents' happiness had even made the news that Mr. Lord had given Lena a pair of ballet shoes for her Christmas box lose its sting.

She sat lost in her plan of campaign. After he had opened the box and been overcome by the beauty of the cake's green-and-white trellis-work icing, she would make her request. Of course, she would do it properly and nicely. And what with the cake and it being Christmas Eve, he would not, of course, refuse her so simple a thing.

Long before they reached Platt's Lane, Mary Ann was on the platform, the box at her feet. When the bus stopped and the conductor lifted the box off and placed it in her arms, she thought for one horrifying moment that she was going to drop it. The conductor's caustic comments followed her as she moved along the road towards the big iron gates. Once there, she propped the corner of the box on a low spike and, panting heavily, rested against it. Then she pushed the other half of the gate open, and when she had passed through she was careful, even under her present difficulties, to follow the same procedure and close it, for it wouldn't do to annoy the Lord this morning. She was actually staggering to the end of the long drive when she saw him coming down the dilapidated broad stone steps of the house.

Mr. Lord's brows had gathered in surprise at the sight of Mary Ann carrying a box as broad as herself and apparently twice as heavy, and it must be admitted that at the sight of him her staggering became so exaggerated as to suggest she was either on a heavy sea or drunk. As neither of these things was possible, it could only be the tremendous weight of the box that was weighting the child down.

The old man moved swiftly towards her, and as Mary Ann relinquished her burden to him with a sigh that was not altogether acting, he demanded, 'Who sent you with this?'

'Me ma,' she gasped.

'Your mother?'

'Yes; it's for you, for Christmas.'

'You mean to say she sent you with this great box? Where's your brother? What's he doing he couldn't bring it, if it had to come?'

Mary Ann remained silent, and Mr. Lord, glancing at her, knew without further explanation why Michael had not been allowed to carry the box and whatever was in it.

And so they entered the house. In the hall they passed Ben, or it would be more correct to say Ben passed them. He passed them as if he were blind, for on no account could Ben be brought on to the side of Mary Ann. To Ben the child was uncanny. Most of his life had been spent with the man who was his master, and there was nothing that he didn't know about him. He knew him to be a hard man and not always just; he was a bitter man and had cause to be; he had for many long years hated women, and children he abhorred, and no female foot had entered these doors for twenty-seven years, until that child came in early one morning. Like a mist she came in, for only a mist could have penetrated the barbed-wire fencing and the high stone walls that bordered the house. Now the gate was left open, the master drove children to school in his car, and, latest madness of all, he was going to build a new house ... at his age! And all this since that child had been allowed in here, that uncanny child who had the temper of a banshee and the coaxing ways of the wee folk. Well, the master could build the house, but would never get him inside it, he would die before that. His usefulness was done. He shambled on into the kitchen.

Mary Ann, standing by the table in the dining room, said 'Aren't you going to open it?'

'What is it?'

'It's your Christmas box from me ma, she made it herself. And you know what?' Her voice sank to an awed whisper. 'There's a glass of brandy in it.'

'Brandy?' he said.

'Yes. Go on, open it and see.'

Mr. Lord somewhat slowly undid the string and opened the box, and lifting the many papers, he unveiled the cake. ·

Mary Ann's eyes had not left his face, and after some time, noticing no ecstatic change taking place, she rose on her toes and peered into the box. Yes, there it was. She cast an eye up at him. 'Isn't it lovely?'

'Yes – yes, very.'

'Me ma made it all herself ... she knew he' – nodding her head as though towards Ben in the kitchen – 'could never manage one. She sent something for him an' all. I've got it here in me pocket; it's three hankies. They were one and elevenpence ha'penny each.'

Mr. Lord turned from contemplating the cake. 'Your mother is very kind – very thoughtful. It's a long time since I had a home-made Christmas cake; or Ben ... any hankies.'

'You'll like it. And she didn't put all marge in either, like ours; she put half butter in yours.'

Slowly Mr. Lord smiled, and putting his hand on her head he wobbled it gently back and forth, and moving towards a chair he guided her to it.

Standing beside his knee she gazed down on his blue-veined hand lying along the arm of the chair and wondered how she would begin to make her request. She took her finger and gently traced a knotted vein to where it disappeared under his cuff, but this meditation gave her no clue.

'What are you going to get for Christmas?'

Quickly now she looked up at him – here was the opening. 'I'm gonna get a school bag and a box of paints, but' – she added, her face taking on a melancholy look – 'that's not what I want.'

'It isn't? What do you want?' He bent over her, his eyes narrowed with inquiry.

'Well, you see, it's a different thing to what you get in your stocking.'

His head came down to hers and he whispered mysteriously, 'I know what it is.'

'You don't,' said Mary Ann.

'I do.'

'What is it then?'

'Ah, that's telling.'

Mary Ann stared at him. He couldn't know, but he was in a fine temper, and that augured only good. 'You can't know,' she said, ''cos I didn't know meself till last night.'

'Oh!' There seemed a trace of disappointment in the old man's face. 'Well, come on, tell me what it is.'

Mary Ann wriggled a little. She hitched up her knickers, which, no matter how tight the elastic might be, would slip down. She put her head first on one side then on the other, then, keeping her eyes lowered and tracing her finger round his hand again, she said, 'You know the house you're going to get built? Well, I know the man who's going to build it.'

Puzzled, Mr. Lord's brows drew together.

'It's Mr. Quinton, isn't it?'

'Yes, but what of it? What's that got to do with your Christmas-box?'

'That's it – that's me Christmas-box. I don't want him to build it.'

Utter perplexity showed in Mr. Lord's face. His turkey neck fell into deeper folds as he drew his chin in; his lips attempted to meet his nose and his eyes became pin points of pale-blue light; but he said nothing – he just waited. And Mary Ann went on, eagerly now, 'That'd be me Christmas-

55

box, if you did that . . . if you got someone else to build your house. I wouldn't want nothing else and I'd do anything for you.'

'Why?'

'Why?'

'Why do you want me to change my builder?'

This was the difficult part. Mary Ann moved uneasily. 'Well, you see, me ma knows Mr. Quinton, and me da . . .'

'Yes?'

'Well, me da . . .'

'Go on.'

'Me da doesn't like Mr. Quinton to be near me ma, and me grannie's always wanting Mr. Quinton to be near her, and—'

Mr. Lord rose, pushing her gently to one side; human triangles always irritated him. The part he himself had played in one had long since ceased to pain him, and people who became so involved were fools. He had been a fool once.

He blew into his moustache and said sharply, 'You must not talk about your parents' affairs.'

'But I can't help it, it's me grannie. . . . Will you get some-body else?'

'No.'

The syllable was final, but Mary Ann refused to recognize it. 'But there's lots of men who build houses.'

'There might be, but I want Mr. Quinton. Now we'll say no more about it. You must not concern yourself about such things, child.' He turned to her again and addressed her gently now. 'Thank your mother for the cake, and come to-morrow and tell me what you get in your stocking.' The last could have been an appeal, but it did not touch Mary Ann.

'I don't want nothing in me stocking.'

Mr. Lord sighed. He had been acquainted with this morsel of humanity for only four months but he recognized only too well the signs of battle.

Mary Ann's mouth was now a button. 'I don't want nothing off you.' Her chin jerked at him.

'Very well.'

'Nothing . . . and I don't care about you buying Lena Ratcliffe ballet shoes.'

Mr. Lord's eyebrows jerked and his face showed surprise at this piece of news. He had certainly given Lena a pound, but ballet shoes. . . .

'She'd never be able to dance in them, anyway, she's too big . . . like a Corporation horse.'

Mr. Lord turned quickly away, saying, 'Well, she can but try.'

'She'd look daft in a ballet dress – she's a pig-face.'

'Now, now.'

'She is. And she's a rotten, swanky, stuck-up . . .'

'Now that's enough, quite enough. And stop shouting.'

'I'm not shouting.'

'Well, if you're not, I never hope to hear you do so.'

'I'm going.'

'Very well.'

'And I'll go to church and ask the Holy Family. They'll stop him building the house for you, you'll see.'

She marched to the door, but no voice bade her come back; not even when she opened the door and halted there did Mr. Lord bid her stay.

In the dim vastness of the hall, she stood pulling at the ends of her woollen gloves with her teeth. Her temper was seeping rapidly away.

Ben, coming from a dark corridor carrying a broom, stopped in his tracks at the sight of her. She turned and, seeing him, remembered the packet in her pocket.

Ben's face was a study as he watched her approach, and whatever his reactions were when she handed him the Christmas-paper wrapped packet, saying flatly, 'Me ma sent you these and she says a Happy Christmas,' he did not allow them to show. But he took the gift from her hand and stood staring at her. She stared back at him. Then, as if he were a confederate, friend, and joint guardian with her of the master of the house, she nodded to him and whispered, 'He's in a bad temper, he won't do nothing.'

There was no word about her own temper, yet her conscience was working at a great rate and she was already thinking, Eeh! I shouldn't have been so cheeky, and after him being so nice and kind and all. I won't half get it if me ma knows.

Ben watched her walk towards the drawing-room door

again, open it quietly and go in, and he looked down on the first wrapped Christmas gift he'd had in years. Slowly he turned and went back into the kitchen again.

In the drawing-room once more, Mary Ann leaned her back against the door and looked towards the forbidding figure standing before the tall window looking out into the wet, unkempt garden.

She coughed; she coughed again. Then, putting her hands behind her, she gently rattled the door handle. But Mr. Lord either did not hear or did not want to hear. Reluctantly leaving the door, she walked slowly up the big room, and skirting the massive table and chairs she came to his side. Once more she coughed, quite loud this time, but its effect was lost and it did not even make him look at her. So, tentatively, with one finger she poked at his coat pocket, and concentrated her gaze on her hand as she said, 'I'm sorry. I didn't mean it.'

There was quite a long pause before he turned and looked down on her. A slight tremor passed over his face but his voice showed no amusement when he said, 'I should hope so.'

He turned and went to the fire, and she followed him saying, 'Are you vexed?'

'No.'

There seemed nothing more to say for a long while. Then, moving nearer to him, she asked, 'Will you be going into Jarrow this mornin'?'

'Yes.'

'Will you take me in with you?'

'Where do you want to go?'

'To church – to pay a visit to the Holy Family . . .' Her voice trailed off as Mr. Lord groped for a chair and sat down – he always had to sit down when he laughed, for that unusual emotion seemed to shake his entire frame.

Mary Ann, pleased and happy at the un-hoped-for turn of events, stood at his knee and joined in his laughter. He was in a good mood and, who knew, he might get another builder . . . he might. She took his hand, and as his laughter rose, her voice vied with his for supremacy. She had only to keep him laughing and everything would be all right.

CHAPTER FIVE

A CHILD IS BORN

WHEN Mary Ann had a project in hand which centred round the happiness of her parents, time itself was ignored. It was only something into which she could cram her efforts. That she was answerable to her parents for what she did with her time was periodically forgotten; it had to be if she wished to achieve anything. Didn't it stand to reason that when every part of her mind, wit and energy was being used on their behalf they should understand? And yet she did not really expect anyone to understand, for people were ... funny, all except her da and Father Owen, and sometimes Mr. Lord.

But with him it was just sometimes, for look at him today and what he had done, or not done. Still laughing, he had left her at the church door, but had damped her spirits with his parting shot: 'This is one time the old firm is not going to help you; you can take my word for that, Mary Ann,' he had said. She knew by the 'old firm' that he meant the Holy Family, and she was downcast by his prophecy. And what was more, he seemed to be right, for she had been unable to get near Jesus, Mary or Joseph at all, not even in her mind.

Inside the church, she had been astonished to see that the group of the Holy Family had been moved, and that in its place stood the Crib. There was some solace, however, in remembering the Star last night and what the Infant had said, but she couldn't get a word in to talk to Him, for there were so many people inside the altar rails messing about with things. There was Miss Honeysett, the priest's housekeeper, and two nuns, and John Findlay and Walter Hewitt, who were altar boys. You couldn't kneel and have a talk with them about, so after saying one desultory 'Our Father' and three equally desultory 'Hail Marys' she went out into the dull, bleak day again, and decided that if she went to see Mrs. McBride she might get a bit dinner. By that time they should have finished messing about with the Crib and she would come back.

Mrs. McBride was delighted to see Mary Ann. Not only did she give her a bit of dinner but kept her for nearly two hours listening to her crack, and when, just on the point of her departure, Mrs. McBride's daughter-in-law and five children swarmed in, Mary Ann was detained yet again and drawn without any hesitation into going out to play Tommy-noddy.

This particular section of Mrs. McBride's grandchildren consisted of four boys and a girl, all under twelve, and all admirers of Mary Ann. What better company in which to meet Sarah Flannagan. And they were no sooner on the street than Sarah made her appearance. She advanced on Mary Ann with slow and deadly intent, exclaiming, 'What you doing here? Get yersel' away, this is our street.'

Mary Ann's courage being greatly reinforced by the McBride squadron, she not only attacked the solitary Sarah with her tongue, but also joined in the fray of pelting her. This game, however, was abruptly brought to a stop by the furious figure of Mrs. Flannagan descending on the gang, as if airborne, and scattering them. Unfortunately, Mary Ann's courage far outstrode her wisdom, and standing to make one last sally at Sarah, she was caught by the scruff of the neck and shaken like a rat by the indignant and enraged lady who, apparently, had heard nothing as yet of 'Peace on Earth to men of goodwill'. If she had she was taking this occasion to prove the utter lack of goodwill towards her and hers by this imp of the devil, for that is what she called Mary Ann. She spoke in so loud a voice that Mrs. McBride was brought to her window, and from there seemingly catapulted into the street and to Mary Ann's defence.

Mrs. McBride was ready to do war with Lady Golightly, as she had nicknamed Mrs. Flannagan, at any season of the year. Very often she didn't wait for an excuse, but were there one to hand it helped to intensify the heat of the battle.

Mary Ann now found herself wrenched from Mrs. Flannagan's hands and almost flung into the middle of the road.

As she saw Mrs. McBride going for Mrs. Flannagan and Mrs. Flannagan looking down her thin nose with utter scorn at the vibrating, wobbling flesh of Fanny, Mary Ann hastily made her retreat and didn't stop running until she had reached Ormond Street, where she tidied her hair, composed herself, and thought, 'Eeh! it's getting dark, I'd better hurry to church, then get the bus home.'

She expected to find the church, at this darkening hour, empty and quietly awaiting her presence and prayers, but instead, to use her own words, it was crushed full. This exaggerated impression was caused by a number of mothers with small children kneeling at various distances from the Crib, waiting to get a better view, and at the other side of the church a number of rows of seats holding scattered penitents waiting to go into Confession in preparation for the Midnight Mass Communion. She stood hesitating near the holy-water font, and definite annoyance filled her – there was a laxity of arrangement somewhere. Here she had, she told herself, been waiting all day to see the Infant Jesus and she was further away from Him than ever. It was no good waiting her turn to get near the Crib, for she'd never be able to talk to Him properly with all these people about, and she'd likely have wilful distractions at prayers, and that'd be a sin, and she'd have to tell it in Confession, and it wouldn't be her fault.

The thought of Confession turned her eyes towards Father Owen's box. That was an idea. Father Owen was next to the Holy Family as the recipient of her troubles. She could talk to him to her heart's content in the confessional box, that is, if she went in last, and she could tell him about everything, even about her da and Mr. Quinton, and her confidence would be as safe as houses. For Mary Ann firmly believed what her imagination and innate desire to shield her father from all censure bid her believe; namely, that God struck a priest blind the minute he entered the confessional box, so that he, not knowing who was talking, would naturally not be able to split on the penitent should he ever be assailed by the desire to do so.

She now went and knelt at the very end of the row, and slowly she moved upwards as, one after the other, the men and women left the pew. But bewilderment filled her when she realized that, as she had been moving up, others had been moving in, and only the fact, although somewhat belated, that she had to get home deterred her from again going to the end of the seat in the hope of being the last. Finally, when it was her turn to go into the box, she realized she had not made any of the usual preparations. But still, she told herself, it didn't really matter, for she hadn't committed any sins, not big 'uns, anyway.

In the dark confessional, with her chin barely reaching the elbow rests, she looked at the dim outline of Father Owen's face which was reflected behind the grid by the light of one candle, and she began her confession. 'Pray, Father, give me thy blessing for I have sinned. It is five days since my last confession.'

There was no word from the priest, so she went on: 'I haven't said me Grace after meals, and I punched me brother and called after Lena Ratcliffe . . . and . . . and . . . I've wanted to push me grannie into the ditch and wished she was dead . . .'

'That's very wicked.'

Mary Ann stared at the grid. He didn't know her grannie; he couldn't know her grannie or he wouldn't have said that.

'Why do you wish your grannie dead?'

'It's because she doesn't like me da, Father, and she's trying to take me ma away from him, like she did afore.'

The priest's head turned sharply, and with his sightless eyes he peered down at Mary Ann. 'What makes you think that?' he asked.

Mary Ann told him why she thought so. Without once mentioning a name she gave him exact details about the building of the house by Mr. Quinton. In fact, she also informed herself, as she talked, of what would happen. It became like a picture unfolding in her mind. She could see Mr. Quinton in their kitchen, and her da coming in and looking mad. . . .

She became so lost in her story that the priest checked her with 'All right, all right.' She stopped and waited, and listened to Father Owen coughing in little short, sharp coughs. Then he said, 'Now you must not worry yourself any more about this matter. Take no heed of it. Why, don't you know what day it is? It's Christmas Eve. Have you been to the Crib?'

'I can't get near it, Father, there's a crush there.'

'Well, go and have another try. Then get off home and to bed, else Santa Claus will be here before you know where you are. What are you going to get in your stocking?'

Somewhat sadly, Mary Ann said, 'A school bag and a box of paints.'

'Well, isn't that what you want?'

'Not very much, Father. I wanted a bike, a two-wheeler, but me ma says it would be years afore I get that, and anyway I'm too little.'

'Ah, you'll grow, and by the time you're ready to reach a bike you'll get one, you'll see. But, anyway, you go and have a talk with the Infant about it, and you can be assured if it's for your good you'll get it. Always remember that ... your tiniest prayer is answered if it's for your good. Now for your penance say three "Hail Marys". Say your act of contrition.'

Mary Ann said the act of contrition and left the box, and, wonder of wonders, the church was nearly empty. Apart from the few people waiting to go into confession, there was no one about, and not a soul at the crib.

Reverently, on tiptoe, she now approached the stable, and it was a real stable, with a donkey and a goat and piles of straw, and there amid the straw sat Our Lady, and there stood Joseph, and there, with hardly a stitch on him, was the Baby. Mary Ann gazed and gazed at Him. In spite of His nakedness He looked warm and snug. She continued to gaze, held spellbound by the wonder of Him. He was lying so quiet; everything in the stable looked quiet. They were all waiting for twelve o'clock, waiting for Him to be born. She found she couldn't pray, or ask anything of Him. He was so little, not at all like He was when seated in His Mother's arms on the altar of the Holy Family.

A lump came into her throat and she sniffed. If she could only touch Him, just a little touch, just put her finger on Him. A quick glance to either side told her she was alone. Trembling, even to her kneecaps, she rose, and skirting the short altar rail she crept up the altar steps. Another three steps and she had passed the imitation rocks and was right

63

behind the donkey. Another quick glance about her to ensure that she was alone, and she knelt down. Now she was looking through the donkey's legs, and there was the Baby, startlingly close but still far away. Four wriggles under the donkey's belly and she was at the side of the Crib.

Heaven and Earth trembled; she was in the stable. There was Our Lady and St. Joseph and the goat, and up above her was the donkey, and before her, in His cradle of straw, was the Baby. Her body shook as her hand went towards Him. When it hovered over His open palm she put out one finger and with a touch like thistledown she rested it on the moulded plaster. The contact was not hard, cold, and lifeless; the warmth from His soft flesh flowed through her little body and made her life His. Like that she stayed for a number of Eternities; then, crawling backwards, she went out the way she had come.

She didn't remember leaving the altar, but as she walked up the aisle she knew she had ... a holy feeling. She could even hear angelic voices singing 'Venite adoremus'. She felt good, in fact, saintly. It may have been the lights from the many candle sconces that danced around her, or it may have been the halo of light that circled round her own saintly head, but she knew she was walking in light and felt ... holy.

History has told us that saints have always been sorely tried, and mostly by their relatives; that they have had to call from time to time on God to fortify their patience when dealing with the ignorance and thick-headedness of members of their families, especially brothers.

Mary Ann, floating in a holy mist out of the church door, was dragged with startling force to earth. 'Where do you think you've been?' Michael, gripping hold of her arm, took on the appearance of the devil himself; but still in her holy state, Mary Ann was proof even against the tempter, and remembering that a gentle word turneth away wrath, she replied in an unnaturally soft voice, 'To the Crib.'

'I've been in church twice for you in the last hour.'

'I was at Confession.' Still the angelic voice.

'Well, don't you think that'll get you off; you're in for it this time.'

'Aw – you!' Like a feather wafted away by a gale of wind,

the holy feeling vanished, and she pulled herself from Michael's hands as he said, 'You had to come straight back home . . . me ma's nearly mad with worry, and on Christmas Eve an' all, and everybody's looking for you.'

'They're not!' She turned on him with scorn. 'Don't tell lies.'

'They are. It's close on six o'clock. Me da's out, and Mr. Lord an' all. Me da's gone to Mrs. McBride's again, and Mr. Lord's taken me ma down to me grannie's.'

'Me grannie's!' Mary Ann's scorn reached the heavens. 'I wouldn't be at me grannie's, would I?'

Michael didn't argue this point, but gripping her firmly by the hand, said, 'Come on. We're all to meet at Ellison Street.'

'Leave go.'

'I won't.'

'If you don't I'll kick your shins, mind.'

'You do if you dare.'

'There then, take that!'

'Oooh! you.' Wincing in pain, Michael released her hand, and she sped away towards Ellison Street with him in hot pursuit.

The light had gone, and with it the holy feeling. She was once more on earth, being buffeted by the ungratefulness of her family. And this was made only too apparent when her da, who was, if the truth be told, really the source of all her troubles, brought her running to a stop by a mighty hand on her shoulder and a mightier voice in her ear demanding the same stupid question, 'Where do you think you've been?'

'To church, Da.'

It seemed for a moment that Mike might explode, he looked so angry, and he almost spluttered as he said, 'You'll do this once too often, mind.'

Standing under the lamp they regarded each other, and Michael regarded them. Then Mary Ann, her head drooping, turned away and looked at the lamp-post, and the three of them stood silent, waiting.

The damp cold was piercing; the only glow of warmth came from the coloured lights in the bar on the opposite side of the street. The bar was decorated gaily, ivy and holly

65

intertwining the bottles on the high shelves, and from it, too, came the sound of laughter and merry talk. Mary Ann's glance slowly raised to Mike. He was staring straight across the street, and in his eyes was that look she knew but could not name. Rapidly now she began to pray for the car to come, and when, in almost immediate answer to her prayer, it drew up close to the kerb in front of them, she forgot she was the culprit and smiled her relief at the occupants. But her smiling was brief, for not only did her mother go for her, but also Mr. Lord as well.

'If it wasn't Christmas Eve,' Lizzie said in a low voice, 'I'd give you the best hiding you ever had in your life.'

'I endorse that, I do firmly.' Mr. Lord stared down on her, and she was almost startled at his ferocity. 'Get in,' he said. 'Never again will I give you a ride. Why didn't you tell me you had to return home? Frightening people.'

She got into the car and sat crouched in the corner, hurt and solitary, listening to their voices all joined together against her. Her da spoke little, but when he did he agreed with Mr. Lord. That was the only solace of the journey.

The misery of last night was past, and the weight that had been placed upon her shoulders, of spoiling everybody's fun, had slid away in sleep.

Jesus was born now – that was her first awakening thought. The next was ... me stocking! She was out of bed and around the curtain that divided her portion of the room from Michael's before she was fully awake, and shaking him by the arm, she hissed, 'Come on, are you coming downstairs?'

Michael, awake at once, muttered, 'Yes, all right; but be quiet.' For him, too, last night was past.

Cautiously, and holding on to each other, they went down the narrow steep stairs to the kitchen. Michael groped for the light, and when it flooded the room they made no dive towards their stockings hanging from the brass rod above the fireplace. Their eyes were glued in hypnotic stares at the table. Even when they moved towards it, they did so slowly. Michael's mouth was agape and Mary Ann's whole expression had taken on the semblance of her ... holy look.

Two shining cycles were propped against the table, one

large and one small, and the labels attached said briefly, 'From Mr. Lord'.

One hand on the seat and one hand holding the label, Mary Ann was still in a state of stupor when Michael was proclaiming his grateful astonishment with gasps and grunts. The label might say from Mr. Lord, but it could only have been at the instigation of the Holy Family that this miracle had been performed, and because of the star last night and her touching the baby. . . .

Michael, in the midst of his joy, glanced at her. Then straightening himself, he exclaimed in astonishment, 'What you crying for now? Oh! you're barmy!'

CHAPTER SIX

A MATTER OF EDUCATION

MIKE pushed his unfinished dinner away from him, and Lizzie, putting down her own knife and fork, asked anxiously, 'What is it? Something's wrong . . . you've been like this for days now.'

Without answering, but passing his hand tightly over his mouth, Mike rose from the table and took his pipe from the mantelpiece. And Lizzie said again, 'Tell me what it is.'

Staring down at the pipe, he said, 'I'm worried, that's all.'

'Is it Ratcliffe?'

'Aye.'

'What has he done?'

'Nothing. . . . Blast them bikes!' He gnawed at his lower lip and thrust his pipe into his pocket.

'But you couldn't help that, Mike.'

'I know, but had I known the old boy wasn't getting Lena one an' all, I wouldn't have accepted them two, seeing how things stood between Ratcliffe an' me. How was I to know he wasn't giving her the same, or something of like value?

It's his fault, he shouldn't make flesh of one and fish of the other. It's a wonder he bought Michael one ... I suppose he couldn't get out of that, being in the same house.'

'Oh, Mike, don't talk like that, he's been so good. We should be grateful.'

'Well I'm not grateful.' Mike spoke quietly and without rancour. 'He does it to buy her, and you know it. And Ratcliffe's taking it out of me because his wife's taking it out of him.'

'But in what way is he doing it; can't you speak about it?'

Mike gave a jerk of his head. He could not tell Lizzie the number of small humiliations he had suffered lately; the dirtiest jobs pushed his way, the placing of a young lad, the latest addition to the farm staff, over him. But the most telling incident had happened yesterday. Coming out of the cattle market after the sale, he had encountered Ratcliffe standing by the best end of the Three Horseshoes. Ratcliffe had looked him straight in the eye and said, 'Coming in for one?' There had been no invitation in the words, only a challenge. Ratcliffe wasn't the kind of boss who drank with his men, but he would have taken him in then and let him drink till he was blind. Mike had been aware, in that instant, that Ratcliffe knew all there was to know about him, and he could date the source of his knowledge from the night Lena had come home and said Mary Ann was fighting with a girl at the bus stop – the writing on the wall had not escaped Lena.

The Ratcliffes were not local people, and Jarrow being six miles from the farm, it was unlikely that his reputation for the bottle would have spread this far. One thing Mike was sure of, Ratcliffe was only waiting his chance to give him the push. And so he would eventually pin something on him, insolence, negligence ... or drink.

He picked up his cap, saying, 'Well, I'll be off.' Then he turned and smiled at her, and she came to him.

'Don't worry; only keep your temper. Promise you will.'

He patted her cheek and laughed. 'I promise I won't hit him.'

He went out, and she stood at the window watching him cross the yard. Why were things made so difficult for him?

He was trying so hard, God knew he was. Not a drop had passed his lips even at Christmas. It was over six months now since he had tasted liquor of any kind. If only he could be given a fair chance and allowed to work peaceably, that was all he asked. But there were so many conflicts raging in and around him. There was Ratcliffe taking it out of him, and Mr. Lord vying with him for Mary Ann – Lizzie admitted to herself what she wouldn't for worlds have admitted to Mike, that Mr. Lord was angling for the child's affection. And she was afraid of the old man's power, the power of his money . . . and his loneliness. Of the two, it was his loneliness that would be the most telling. It even affected herself. She knew Mr. Lord's history, as did everyone in and around Jarrow. Except for going daily to the shipyard, he had lived like a hermit for years. Some of the older folk remembered the big splash his wedding had made, when at past forty he married a girl less than half his age, and spent so much on her whims that he nearly went broke. And then she had left him. Now in his old age, Mary Ann had brought him back to life and he saw in her what might have been had he been given a child to rule and mould, and in whose affection he could warm his thinning blood.

But that a child of his would not have resembled Mary Ann in the least, Mr. Lord did not consider, for he thought he saw in Mary Ann's tenacity of purpose and courage a reflection of himself. This, coupled with her being so endearing, made her almost irresistible to him.

Sensing all this, Lizzie saw a bitter struggle ahead. But its end she would not even try to see.

Mike had long since passed from her sight, and she was about to turn from the window when two moving figures on the hill opposite caught her attention. She knew them both. One was the man who had been filling her mind for the past few minutes and the other was a man who had filled her early life, the unformed years of her teens. Even when the image of the red-headed farm boy had occupied her nightly dreams, her waking thoughts, guided by her mother, had seen in Bob Quinton not only a husband but a man who was going to rise. Bob had risen, beyond even his own dreams, and he hadn't married. . . . She turned from the window.

It was many months now since she had seen him. The last

time was the night he had kindly given her a lift home from the bus stop, only to be seen by Mike. The repercussion of the events of that evening had resulted in Michael almost killing himself. She turned her mind from it now and from the man himself, and busied herself with clearing the table and washing-up.

She was sitting by the fire, hurriedly finishing off a pair of socks for Michael before the light of the short afternoon should fade, when there came a knock on the back door, and on opening it she was faced by the two men.

She did not look at the tall, pleasant-faced, fair man or give him any greeting. It was to Mr. Lord she looked and spoke: 'Won't you come in?' she said.

'Thank you; we will for a moment. This is my builder ... I understand you know each other?'

'Hallo, Elizabeth.'

'Hallo, Bob. Will you take a seat? It's very cold out.' There was restraint in her voice.

'Yes, it's nippy. No, I won't sit down. You're looking very well, Elizabeth, farm life agrees with you. How are the children?'

'Oh, excellent.'

The exchange of pleasantries was all very stilted and correct.

As Mr. Lord's glance moved quickly from one to the other, he thought, Fool of a woman ... women are all fools. They would have made a fine pair, if there is such a thing ... and she would have had an easy mind.

'May I get you a cup of tea?' asked Lizzie. But both men answered together 'No, no.'

As she stood in an uneasy calm by the side of the table, Bob looked at her with the penetrating look she knew so well. During times of heartache in the past she had thought of this look, but now it embarrassed her. She pulled a chair forward. 'Do sit down,' she said.

'Thanks all the same, Elizabeth, but I'm due in Newcastle in fifteen minutes. I just wanted to come in and say hullo.' He glanced at his watch. 'Yes, I must make a move, but I'll be seeing you again, that's sure.'

The 'that's sure' disturbed her, although she knew it meant nothing. It was as natural for him to be nice and pleasant as it was for Mike to be hot-headed, but Mike would read a personal meaning into every gesture Bob was likely to make in her presence.

'Good-bye, sir,' he said to Mr. Lord. 'Good-bye, Elizabeth; remember me to the children.'

He had not mentioned Mike. Well, it was to be understood. She went to the door with him, and there he did not repeat his farewells but smiled at her quietly before leaving. The smile was disturbing, and she returned to the kitchen thinking: Pray God Mike and he never come in together.

'I want to discuss something with you, Mrs. Shaughnessy.'

'Yes, Mr. Lord.' Lizzie seated herself on the opposite side of the hearth and looked at the old man. Even with the kindly note in his voice he appeared forbidding, and she marvelled once again how Mary Ann had ever got round him.

'I am going to come to the point, Mrs. Shaughnessy. I don't believe in a lot of palaver.'

Lizzie waited.

'It's about the child.'

A queer little pain touched her just below her ribs; it tightened the muscles and caused her to take a deep breath.

'Her education.'

Still Lizzie waited.

'I want to have her educated – properly educated; sent away to a good school right away from all this.' He waved his hand about the room, yet his meaning excluded it but encompassed the whole of the Tyne.

'No.' Lizzie stood up.

'Why do you say no without even considering the matter?'

'Her father – he wouldn't hear of that . . . not for her to go away.'

'If it's for the child's good . . .?'

'He would miss her so.'

'He won't be the only one. Don't think I haven't given the matter thought.' He paused and turned his eyes from her and looked into the fire. 'I'm fond of the child.'

'Yes, yes, I know.' Lizzie was breathing heavily. 'Then

71

why want to send her away, there are plenty of fine schools about here?'

'There may be, but not for her. Don't you see, woman, if she were near, the pull of you and him, and even me, would interfere with any form of higher education.'

For a moment Lizzie's shoulders went back as she faced the autocratic figure. 'I don't want Mary Ann changed, not fundamentally.'

'Don't you want her to have the chances you have dreamed of?' He turned further round in his chair. 'You are an intelligent woman, Mrs. Shaughnessy. With the right sort of education you could have gone far. Think of Mary Ann at your age. What will she be if left where she is now?'

'It's quite a good school.'

'For some it might be . . . not for Mary Ann. She hardly knows anything. She hasn't the faintest knowledge of English, her grammar makes me squirm. She uses "us" instead of "we". Everything is "me this", "me that", and "us has got". Its criminal in a child of her intelligence.'

'She'll get out of all that; children do.'

'They don't . . . most of them get worse once they leave school. "Ganging hyem", they say. "Had on", they say. You know they do. Do you want her to speak like that?'

'I don't think it matters very much how one speaks, it's how one acts that counts.'

'Don't be silly, woman.' He stood up. 'They act mostly as they speak.'

Lizzie put her hand to her trembling lips. 'I know you mean well, sir, and you have been kindness itself to us all, but I would ask you to forget about this and leave Mary Ann where she is. In any case, it's hopeless – Mike will never agree to it.'

'Mike!' Mr. Lord's head swung from his shoulders as if it would leave his body; it was as if Mike's name had set his nerves jangling. 'Look, I'll have this settled now – send for him. He's no fool about the child, no matter what else he is. He will put her first.'

Lizzie put her hand on the table and steadied herself. 'It's no use, sir; besides, there's no one here to go for him.'

'Then I'll soon find someone.'

She watched him march out of the cottage, and to her amazement she heard him imperiously request Mrs. Jones to bring Mike at once. She sat down as if to give herself respite before the coming battle. The old man, she could see, was on his high horse, when he would brook no interference from anyone. But Mike wasn't anyone, he was Mary Ann's father. He was her life-spring, and she, to a great extent, was his. They couldn't do without each other. Mike's words came back: 'He does it to buy her.' He was right.

Mr. Lord returned and sat down, but did not speak. The room, warm and still, took on the atmosphere of a court room where the judge, who was also the prisoner, was awaited.

Even as they fought they jumped about, clapped their hands and stamped their feet to ward off the penetrating cold. Sarah and her army of three were ranged on one side, while Mary Ann with only Cissy and Agnes were on the other.

'You think you're everybody because you've been picked to say poetry,' said Sarah, skipping in an imaginary rope. 'Any fool can learn poetry.'

'Then why don't you?' said Mary Ann pertly.

' 'Cause I wouldn't want to be like you, for all the tea in China, because you're the biggest liar from here to Frenchmen's Bay and back – telling people that the Infant Jesus brought you that bike.'

'I didn't say that, so there.' Mary Ann bounced her head at the grim-visaged Sarah. 'I said that I prayed to Him and He told Mr. Lord to get it . . . Father Owen told me to do it. "Go on and ask the Baby, Mary Ann," he said, "and He'll give you anything you want because He knows you're good." That's what he said. So there!'

Thumping her forehead with her fist, Sarah turned amazed eyes to her followers, and together they followed her example and thumped their own heads. 'She's barmy!' cried Sarah. 'She'll end up in the looney bin.'

'I'll not,' said Mary Ann, blowing on her gloved hands, 'but I know where you'll go for certain – Hell – down there!' She thumbed the earth. 'Hell! Hell! Hell!' Each word was emphasized with a jump, and on the loudest 'Hell!' and the highest jump, a voice said: 'Mary Ann Shaughnessy! you come to me in the morning.'

The injustice meted out by teachers in general and this one in particular kept Mary Ann, in spite of the intense cold, immovable as she watched the departing figure. Then a splutter from Sarah brought her round in fury: 'You! you great big goat-face! I'll tell me da on you,' she cried.

'I'll tell me da on you,' mimicked Sarah. 'Me da's a grand man.'

'So he is, an' all.'

'And a grand drinker.'

Still mimicking, Sarah turned on her heel with this shot, and taking her friends with her, ran out of the school yard, with Mary Ann's voice helping her on her way, crying, 'Oh you! you . . . you big liar! You'll burn in . . .' She stopped abruptly and glanced round, but there were only the questioning eyes of her friends upon her. 'She's jealous of me bike,' she ended lamely. Then, 'Come on,' she said, 'else I'll miss the bus. And' — she added, by way of payment to her reserve army — 'I'll give you a ride on me bike when the weather's fine and me ma lets me ride it.'

By the time Mary Ann reached the bus stop she was once more in harmony with her own particular world, for she had regaled her admiring friends with the wonders of the farm: their cottage, which had now reached the proportions of a mansion house; Mr. Lord, who was the good genie and bestower of all gifts; but lastly and covering all, her da and his high position on the farm.

She waved to her friends from the bus, and they waved back, even running along the streets to get a last glimpse of her from the window. She was happy. And wait till her da knew she had been picked from the whole school to say poetry at the monthly assembly, when all the classes would be there. Wasn't it lucky she had been asked to recite bits from Hiawatha? She liked Hiawatha because it was sing-songy.

To the rhythmic purr of the bus she began to recite to herself from Hiawatha's Childhood, shaking her head each time she repeated the plea of the animals and birds, 'Do not shoot us, Hiawatha,' until she reached the end and rendered triumphantly to herself,

> *'All the village came and feasted,*
> *All the guests praised Hiawatha,*
> *Called him Strong-Heart, Soan-ge-taha!*
> *Called him Lion-Heart, Mahn-go-taysee!'*

But long before the bus reached the cross-roads her thoughts had sunk to a less literary level and she was endeavouring to compose a rhyme that would make Sarah Flannagan mad. Line after line was discarded as not bad enough, and by the time the bus stopped she had given up the attempt. But she still felt happy; so, to the rhythm of

> *'Boxy, boxy, push it down your socksy;*
> *Umper, umper, push it up your jumper,'*

she hitched down the lane home.

'Boxy, boxy' was a very good thing to hitch to – it got you along – and so happy was she to be home that she continued to chant in no small voice right across the yard and into the scullery, but stopped dead at the kitchen door.

In the kitchen, and all looking at her, were her ma and da and Mr. Lord, and she did not need her eyes to tell her that there had been a row. The atmosphere was enough. The tension conveyed itself to her and touched her nerves like a vibrating wire.

'Say that again.'

'What?' She looked at Mr. Lord.

'That jingle you were saying as you came in.'

Mary Ann looked from Lizzie to Mike, then at Mr. Lord again, and she repeated slowly and flatly, 'Boxy, boxy, push it down your socksy; umper, umper, push it up your jumper.'

It didn't sound right like that, you had to hitch to it.

Mr. Lord turned on Mike. 'The school is good enough for her, she is learning fast! That's what she is learning.'

Mike's face was unusually pale. He wet his lips a number of times before saying, 'Look, sir, let's get this straight once and for all. She's my daughter, she'll have the education I can afford and that's all.'

There was almost a sneer on Mr. Lord's face. 'And what do you pay for her present education?'

'Nothing,' barked Mike, with startling suddenness, 'and that's what I can afford!'

Lizzie closed her eyes and her hand went to her throat as she waited, but unexpectedly Mr. Lord did not answer Mike with a similar bark. His voice became even quieter. 'Look,' he said, 'will you let her decide for herself?'

'No – a child of her age doesn't know what she wants.'

'True in most cases, but this case I think is different. She knows what she wants, if anybody does. Will you take a chance on it? I promise you I'll stand by it, and you won't hear me mention the matter again if it goes against me.'

Lizzie brought Mike's eyes to hers, and he saw the fear in them, not of Mary Ann being allowed to choose, but of his reactions to this affair no matter what the child's choice should be. Fear for him was ever present with Lizzie, and nothing he ever did seemed to allay it. The anger that was boiling in him suddenly lost its intense heat. 'All right,' he said, 'have it your way.'

Now they all looked at Mary Ann, but no one offered to tell her what she had to choose, and she gazed from one to the other in troubled perplexity. Heavily, Lizzie moved towards her, and, taking her hand, drew her to a chair. She sat down and brought Mary Ann to face her squarely, and in a low voice began to talk to her as one does to a child when another is asleep.

'You know the stories you read in your *Girl's Own* and *The Schoolgirl* about the big schools where the girls sleep in dormitories and have parties at the end of term before they go home?'

'Yes, Ma.'

'Do you like those stories?'

'Yes, Ma.'

Lizzie paused and looked away from Mary Ann to Mr. Lord's feet. They were thin feet, she noticed, long and thin. He was all long and thin, not capable surely of such tenacity to a whim, for that's all it was, a whim.

She looked at Mary Ann again. 'You know at those schools the girls learn different things from what you do at your school?'

'Yes, Ma. But' – Mary Ann brightened a little – 'I've been

76

picked for poetry, I'm going to say Hiawatha before the whole school, and Sarah Flannagan ...'

'Yes, yes, you can tell me later. I'm glad you've been picked. But listen – would you like to learn French and German, and play hockey?'

'Oh yes, Ma.'

Lizzie paused again – she dare not look at Mike – 'And talk properly?'

Now Mary Ann's bewilderment vanished. She became herself again. Her chin edged upwards, just the slightest and she inquired in no meek voice, 'Like Lena Ratcliffe?'

'Something like Lena – perhaps better.'

Mary Ann turned and glanced at Mr. Lord. Then she asked, 'Grammar and things?'

'Yes.'

'I don't want to be like Lena Ratcliffe, but. ...' She paused. There was another side to this. Imagine being able to talk swanky and boast about your house matches to Sarah Flannagan, like Gwendolyn Tremayne did in *The Prefect of the Fourth*. She would say to her, in her best swanky voice, 'So you see, Sarah Flannagan, I'm a prefect, and you've got to do as I say or I'll have you chucked out – no, thrown out, on your great big ugly mug, and ...'

'You'll have to go a long way from home and only come back in the holidays.'

Only come home in the holidays. ... Mary Ann swung round and looked at Mike. He was staring at her, but she could get nothing from his face. It looked blank, as if he was asleep with his eyes open. If she went to this school she wouldn't see him, not for weeks and weeks. She wouldn't hear him laughing, she wouldn't be here to pour the water over his head when he washed, and she always poured the water over his head, and when he was sad and had his gone-away look she wouldn't be here to make him laugh. And she wouldn't see her ma or their Michael either. Suddenly the thought of not seeing Michael became painful, too, in spite of the fact that last night he had punched her because she had slapped him on the back with the cold, wet flannel when he was taking off his shirt. Everything quite suddenly became painfully dear to her. Above all, far above all, the dearness of her da. Yet, as her answer came into her mind, her head drooped, for there came over her a feeling of pity for Mr. Lord. He was nice, in spite of his growling when he talked, and he was kind, and she would like to please him, 'cos hadn't he bought her that bike. But if she pleased him, she would displease her da.

'I don't want to go to any school if I have to go away.'

Neither Mike nor Mr. Lord moved, nor did their expressions change. Lizzie, glancing from one to another, and relief rising in her, made herself say, 'Now are you sure? Remember you will have nice clothes and meet nice girls.'

'But I don't want to – not to go away.'

Mr. Lord picked up his hat from the chair and without a word made for the door, and before Lizzie could rise to open it he was gone.

Mary Ann went towards Mike. She felt all of a sudden quiet and somehow tired. She leant against his leg and his hand moved gently on her hair.

'Get your things off,' said Lizzie; and to Mike she said, 'Are you going back now before your tea?'

'Yes, I'm going back now.' He spoke quietly; then he eased Mary Ann from his leg and went out.

'Get your hands washed,' said Lizzie.

Mary Ann washed her hands. Everything was as it had been, except that she felt sorry for Mr. Lord.

CHAPTER SEVEN

THE LAPSE

'AND you know what I said to him next, Mrs. McBride?'

'No.' Fanny pushed her folded arms, which supported her huge breasts, further on to the table. 'Go on, hinny, and tell me; me ears are like cuddy's lugs.'

'Well' – Mary Ann became lost in recalling the scene of three weeks ago – 'well, I said to him: I'm not going to your fancy school, cos I don't want to be a lady and talk posh and swanky, an' I said I'm gonna stay home with me ma and da.'

'And what did the old boy say to that?' Fanny's eyes were lost in deep wrinkles of amusement.

'Oh, he said lots, he kept on and on and on.'

'And you wouldn't give in?'

'No.'

'Good for you. You stick to your ma and da.'

'I'm going to.' Mary Ann now also leaned her elbows on the table. It was nice being in Mrs. McBride's kitchen, although it wasn't clean like theirs for it smelt of onions and soapsuds and baking herrings; and it was nice being with Mrs. McBride, for she made you feel fine and important, and she took away all the things that kept niggling inside of you. She had even dulled the one terrifying thing, the fear. Yet the terrifying thing itself seemed more at home now in this house than it did in the cottage, for it had nearly happened here last year, and now it was starting again. She had no name for it, this thing which existed between her ma and da and Mr. Quinton, but just a fortnight ago it had come into their lives again. She had seen it almost take on tangible form and fill the kitchen, when her da walked in upon her ma and Mr. Quinton having a cup of tea, and her ma had the best cloth on and the good china out, and it was Saturday and the men weren't working on the house. Mr. Quinton had spoken nicely to her da and her da had spoken nice back, but even as they walked about the house the terrifying thing was there. Yet it did not leap to real life until her ma and da went to bed, when they fought quietly, their words hissing unintelligibly, well into the night.

The next day her ma's face was stiff and white. And then there was yesterday and the snow-balling. Her and their Michael were pelting their ma with snowballs in the lane when Mr. Quinton came along – he was walking, because he couldn't get his car up the lane – and he joined in the fight, helping their ma, and they all had a rare game; and nobody came past, only Mr. Ratcliffe. Yet her da knew, because when he came in he said, 'Well, did you have some fine sport?' and it wasn't really to her and Michael he said it but to their ma. And this morning her face was all white again.

And then straight after dinner her da had gone out. That's why she was here.

In the soothing company of this fat, grubby old woman she had forgotten for the moment why she had been sent into Jarrow. Lizzie, in her agony of uncertainty as to what Mike in the throes of his jealousy might do, had sent Mary Ann to his old haunt in the hope, not that she might find him sober, but that, with the usual power the child had over him, she might induce him to return home quietly, for Mike, under the influence, was a one-man show. Beer did not make him belligerent but gave him the desire to entertain. Contrary to his attitude towards the mass in his sober state, when in drink he sought out his fellows, and with song and dance regaled them. It was this regaling that filled Lizzie with shame and gave a sourness to Mike's own awakening.

'And what are you in Jarrow for the day on your own?' inquired Mrs. McBride. And when Mary Ann, with a betraying nonchalance, said, 'Oh, just to look round,' Mrs. McBride squinted at her and drew her chins in, fold upon fold.

'Just to look round!' she said.

'M'm.'

The squint became narrower. 'Don't tell me Mike's at it again.'

The blood rushed to Mary Ann's face.

'Dear God, is he mad? To jeopardize a fine job! What's come over him this time?'

Mary Ann stood up. 'He hasn't done it . . . I mean I just come to look for him.' Then her small show of defiance slid away. This old woman knew all there was to know – hadn't she saved their Michael's life after he gassed himself, and didn't she like her da and always stood up for him? She said quietly, 'He went out all on his own, and he usually takes us on a Saturday, and me ma was worried and sent me to look for him. And I waited till the Ben Lomond came out and he wasn't there; nor at the Long Bar; nor at Rafferty's.'

'He's a blasted fool if ever there was one!' cried Fanny indignantly. 'And old Lord won't stand for him and the bottle again. He should tread warily there.'

This last remark put into words another worry. Everyone had to tread warily with Mr. Lord now; he wasn't like he used to be. He didn't pass the cross-roads in the morning and give them all a lift to school, and he never came into their house at all now; and he had refused to take her hand that day in the farmyard. And Lena Ratcliffe had seen and had crowed over her the next morning.

'You're being put in your place,' she had said, 'and Mammie says it's not before time.'

When she had jumped at Lena and slapped her face she had expected their Michael to go for her, but strangely enough he didn't, he went for Lena instead. That had made her feel . . . funny towards him, and that night she had lent him her paint-box.

'Look, get on your coat and get off to the bus and away home, and it's ten to one you'll find him there, solid and sober . . . Well, it's to be hoped to God you will, anyway,' added Fanny.

After buttoning Mary Ann up to the eyes against the biting, snow-filled wind, Fanny pushed a packet of bullets into her pocket and sixpence into her hand, and setting her to the top of the steps, called a cheery farewell to her. Mary Ann's farewell was equally cheery, but as soon as she was out of the old woman's sight her cheeriness vanished.

Cold as she was, both inside and out, and filled with longing to get home to see if her da was back, she made her way to the church. Her misery seemed to draw her there. There was no Crib today, no glowing lights, in fact the Holy Family looked perished to the bone themselves, for there wasn't even one candle lit to keep them warm. And there was no heat from the hot-water pipes – they weren't on, as hers and hundreds of other sets of chattering teeth had confirmed only yesterday morning, for there had been a burst.

Before kneeling down, she lit one candle, with tuppence left from her pocket money; then slowly withdrawing the newly acquired sixpence, she gazed at it. The silver piece represented a comic, two ounces of shelled monkey nuts and a single stick of spearmint. She could make these entertaining purchases on her way home, and the night after she was bathed all over she could sit on the fender close to the fire and read her comic while she chewed her nuts. And in bed, so that her ma wouldn't see, she could chew the spearmint and make bubbles with it – she was a dandy hand at making bubbles with gum. But would she do all this if her da was . . . sick? The answer came with the tinkle of the sixpence as it fell into the tin box.

She had not consciously decided to devote this enormous sum to the benefit of the Holy Family. But it was done now, so she took up three more candles. She had never lit four candles at one go in her life before, but this was an emergency, and she hoped that the Holy Family would appreciate that fact. They did so immediately, for they all looked warmer. Saint Joseph smiled quietly at her and his smile thanked her.

Kneeling down before them, she began, 'Please, Jesus, Mary and Joseph, I can't stay a minute because I've got to catch the bus. I only come into Jarrow to look for me da, but I was so cold I went in to Mrs. McBride's to get a warm. I didn't find me da. Please, oh please, Jesus, Mary and Joseph you can stop doing anything for me, you can make me bad and have the 'flu or let me fall down or let me teacher go for me or even Sarah Flannagan get one on me, but please don't let me da start to get . . . sick again. Oh, please!'

The candles, in a draught of air, flickered wildly, the statues moved and the Virgin hitched the Infant further up into her arms before bending forward and saying, 'Go home; everything will be all right.'

The candle flames steady once more, Mary Ann blessed herself, then rose and went out. She felt sort of empty and quiet inside. It was a relieved sort of feeling, but it did not cause her to feel boisterous, she did not want to run, skip or jump. She walked decorously to the bus stop, boarded the bus, sat quietly in the corner seat, and so came home.

And it was as the Holy Family had said – there he was, solid and sober, sitting before the fire. He had on his good suit and he looked nice, but not happy.

As she entered the door a signal passed between Mary Ann and Lizzie, and the signal said, 'Say nothing; don't tell him where you've been.' But as her da looked at her, Mary Ann knew that he knew where she had been – it was in his eyes like a deep hurt.

It was nearly a fortnight later when Mary Ann learned

where her da had been that Saturday afternoon, he had been after another farm job. This had distressed her, for she told herself, I like it here, and our nice house; and I wouldn't see Mr. Lord again. Though this last should not have troubled her, for he was still nasty, and never spoke to her. She had followed him one Saturday morning when he had gone up the hill to see his house. It was slowly rising from its foundations, and she had stood quite near him and offered her opinion. 'It's nice,' she had said, 'and you're gonna have a lot of windows, aren't you?' But he had only grunted; and after a while she had walked away because she wanted to cry. But she had stopped herself by saying, 'He's a bad-tempered, nasty old beast.' And when he had come down the hill to his car she had kept close, but not too close, and, just to let him see she didn't care, she had skipped with her ropes to 'Boxy, boxy, stick it down your socksy'. But he had suddenly yelled at her, 'Stop that!' and she had stopped and stared at him, and he had got into his car and banged the door and gone off.

Mr. Lord had just this minute gone from the cowshed. She was keeping out of his way, staying up in the loft until he was well passed. He was talking now to Mr. Ratcliffe about Clara. Clara was going to have a baby, and when Mary Ann heard Mr. Lord mention her da's name she nearly fell out of the loft, straining to hear what he had to say. Only the tail end of it came to her: 'If there should be any trouble, let Shaughnessy deal with her.'

There was no response from Mr. Ratcliffe that Mary Ann could hear, and preening with pride she nodded in the direction of the departing men. That was one in the eye for Mr. Ratcliffe. Mr. Lord wanted her da to see to Clara because he was a right fine man with cows, and Clara had been bad and had had the doctor.

She came down from the loft and went into the cowshed. Her da wasn't there. There was no one there except Clara and Mr. Jones. Clara looked very large, very soft and very warm. Mr. Jones looked very small, very hard, and his expression was anything but warm as he stared at her. Mr. Jones and Mary Ann were not on speaking terms. Mr. Jones's memory was long and his sense of humour only really active when he himself was the cause of its rising.

She came out of the cowshed and went to the pigsties. Her da wasn't there, either, only Joe and their Michael. Michael looked happy. He was whistling, and she said to him, 'Have you seen me da?'

'Yes,' he said, 'he's just gone up to mend the fence in the long field. And you know what' – his voice fell, and he leaned nearer to her over the sty wall – 'he's going to let me keep one of Daisy's puppies.'

'Oh goody – if it's a girl I'll call it Pat.'

'You'll call it nothing of the kind, it's gonna be mine.'

The usual relations were resumed, and Mary Ann cried, 'Aw – you! it won't be all your dog – I'll ask me da.'

Michael's voice followed her as she sped out of the yard and up the lane.

The long field lay some way beyond the cottages, and it was a chance glance when speeding past them that brought her to a dead stop. The cottage door which led into the scullery was open, and standing outside round the corner under the lean-to was her da. Mary Ann herself was so versed in the art of listening that she recognized immediately that that was what her da was doing. After a long moment during which she presented to herself many reasons for her da's eavesdropping but would not allow herself to think of the true one, she moved towards him, walking softly, and she was within a few feet of him before he became aware of her presence. And when he did he ordered her away, but silently. With a quick movement of the head and hand he bid her be gone, and he looked as if he were about to enforce this when the low, pleasantly deep voice of Bob Quinton came from just beyond the door. It stiffened Mike's half-turned body, and Mary Ann's eyes, riveted on his profile, actually say the colour drain from it and leave it looking like dirty snow as Mr. Quinton's voice came to them, saying, 'You know, Elizabeth, there was only you. All those years there was only you.' She wanted to dash to the door and bang it, or yell and shout so that her da wouldn't hear any more, but as if anticipating this move, Mike's hand pressed back on her.

The sound of Bob's voice still came to them, but his words now were not audible. Then there followed a silence that filled Mary Ann's mind with wild pictures, and she saw the silence stretch her da's body until she thought his head would shoot up through the corrugated roof. She knew that in another second he would fling himself into the house and hit Mr. Quinton. It was then her ma's voice came, whispering softly, and instead of adding impetus to Mike's taut limbs it seemed as if Lizzie's hushed words drew the very sinews out of them. 'It makes me happy, Bob, to hear you say that,' she was saying. 'I've waited a long time for you to tell me that . . . I've prayed for it.'

That's what her ma had said. The words themselves held no particular meaning – it was the nice way her ma had said them that gave Mary Ann the feeling that her own slight body was shrinking. The earth shuddered under her feet, the trees swayed, and the heavens became tilted. She closed her eyes against a rocking world, and when she opened them her da had moved.

Mary Ann had witnessed all kinds of emotions on Mike's face, from such gentleness that made her cry to tearing rage that terrified her. She had seen him look lost and pitiful, but never had she seen him look as he was doing now, like a blind man. And like a blind man he put his hand out and touched the post of the lean-to and stood for the moment looking away up the hill to the house Mr. Quinton was building. Then he lifted his shoulders, pressing them back until his back, turned towards Mary Ann, was straight as a die, and like that he walked towards the long field.

Mary Ann went across the yard to the lavatory, and through the air holes in the door she watched Mr. Quinton take his leave and her ma smile at him with her nice smile. When the yard was empty once more she still continued to strain up and look through the holes as though she were fixed there. Then, as if she had been suddenly cut down, she dropped on to the seat and, pressing her hands tightly between her knees, she rocked herself, muttering, 'Eeh! no. Eeh! no.' One part of her mind refused to believe what the other half was telling her – her ma was bad.

She came out from the lavatory and, without glancing towards the cottage, she went up the road to the long field. Mike was mending the fence and from a distance he looked as he did on any other day. She did not go near him. She knew she could not bear to see his hurt at close quarters, but she watched him from the side of the gate until he finished the job, and when he went back to the farmyard she went slowly into the house. She felt drawn there – to look at her ma and see how changed she was.

But Lizzie wasn't changed, except that she looked happier. She was actually humming to herself. After one searching glance, Mary Ann turned towards the fire, and Lizzie, who was ironing on the table, said, 'I'm nearly finished. Put the dinner plates on top of the oven and then you can set the table.' She didn't look towards her daughter, but seemed preoccupied with her own thoughts.

Mary Ann did as she was bidden. She did it quickly, because she wanted to get out again; she didn't want to be in when her da came in.

Fifteen minutes later she was standing behind the stone pillar that had once supported a gate to the farmyard. She wanted to see her da come out without him seeing her. She saw him pass into the road, but he didn't turn up towards the lane which led to the back door of the cottages, or keep on the main road which led to the front door, but he jumped the fence bordering the field opposite the gate.

Her mouth agape, she watched him striding along the outskirts of the field. She wanted to shout after him, but she couldn't, there was no voice left in her. All expression for the moment was weighed down with the awful knowledge that her da was making for the bus and Jarrow ... and the Ben Lomond, or some other bar, and with him he was taking all his week's wages. The men usually got paid on a Friday night, but Mr. Ratcliffe had been away all day yesterday at a cattle sale and he would have paid the men this morning. She put a hand across her mouth to stop the moaning sound that was escaping, then, running like the wind, she went home. Gone now was the thought that her ma was bad. Bursting into the kitchen, she gasped, 'Me da! he's got on the bus.'

Lizzie looked at her dumbfounded. 'Your da?' she said. 'What bus?'

'For Jarrow.'

'Jarrow?' Lizzie repeated stupidly. She stared at Mary Ann, and Mary Ann stared back at her. She was now feeling bewildered at the expression of her mother, who looked absolutely stunned. 'But why?' she muttered.

86

Mary Ann turned her head away, then her body, and stared at the table leg; only to be swung furiously about. 'What is it?' Lizzie demanded.

Mary Ann looked hard at her mother for a moment before saying, 'He heard – when you were with Mr. Quintin – in the scullery.'

'My God!'

Lizzie stood back from her daughter. Her fingers went to her lips, and for the moment Mary Ann thought she was going to burst into tears. But she didn't. Instead, going to her purse, she grabbed a shilling out of it and, thrusting it into Mary Ann's hand, cried, 'Look. Go on after him, tell him to come home. Tell him' – she passed her hand over her face and drew in a long breath – 'tell him Mr. Quinton is going to be married.'

'Married, Ma? Oh!' Relief gushed into Mary Ann's body, and so activated her limbs that she was out of the door and halfway across the yard before she pulled up, swung on her heel and retraced her steps.

'It's nearly another half-hour afore the next bus, Ma.'

Lizzie seemed to become smaller. She sat down heavily on a chair, and Mary Ann stood gazing pitifully at her, until, rousing herself, she said, 'I'd better go myself.'

'No, no, Ma' – Mary Ann pressed her back – 'he'll come for me . . . and quiet. I'll bring him. Look; I'll run to Morpeth Lane, the Shields bus that goes down Robin Hood way passes there. That'll take me.'

'Go on then,' said Elizabeth. 'And run.'

Mary Ann ran, and as she neared the corner of Morpeth Lane she screamed and yelled and waved her arms as she saw the bus speeding away from her. Then, as if by a miracle, it stopped some way down the road, and she stumbled on to it almost in a state of collapse.

A woman, lifting her on to the seat, said, 'You shouldn't run like that, hinny, there's other buses.'

Mary Ann said nothing, only pressed her hand to her side to ease the stitch.

When she left the bus she ran again, along streets, up back lanes, down alley-ways, across main roads, until she came to the Ben Lomond; and there she stopped and waited, for she could not see inside the bar and she dared not open the door.

But when a man came out, she asked him, 'Is me da there? He's Mr. Shaughnessy ... Mike Shaughnessy. Will you tell him to come out a minute, please?' And the man, pushing open the door, called, 'Anybody by the name of Shaughnessy here? Mike Shaughnessy?'

It was the bar-man's voice which answered, 'Mike Shaughnessy? No, he's not here. Haven't seen Mike for weeks. Who wants him?'

'His bairn.'

'Oh well, tell her he's not here.'

'He's not in there, hinny,' said the man.

'Ta,' said Mary Ann, and walked away.

He might be in the Long Bar. ... Running again, she came to Staple Road and the Long Bar, and here she followed the same procedure, and with the same result. She stood on the edge of the pavement blinking down at the muddy gutter. It was nearly one o'clock. She would go to Rafferty's, and if he wasn't there she would go home, and like that other Saturday she would find him sitting in the kitchen, but happy now because Mr. Quinton was going to be married.

At Rafferty's, her meeting with two men coming out of the bar took all thought of speeding home from her. Yes, they said, Mike Shaughnessy had been in, but he had gone not ten minutes ago.

'Where?' she asked.

That they couldn't say, but she could try the Long Bar.

She went back to the Long Bar; she went back to the Ben Lomond. He had been to neither. So she now started a round of the other bars, foreign places, because she had never before stood outside them. She paraded High Street from the Wellington to the Duke of York, and then to the Telegraph. Outside the small bar stood a number of people. They were in groups, and the groups informed Mary Ann that in one way her search was ended, for it was closing time. She did not ask if anyone had seen her da, but stood against a house windowsill and rested for a moment. She was very tired, her legs ached and she felt sick.

There was no thought in her mind now of going home. Her da had been in the bar; and from one he would have gone to another, on and on till closing time, and even then he wouldn't go straight home – her da liked a bit of jollification when he was full. She moved from the wall. It would be easier finding him now anyway. She just had to walk until she heard somebody singing out loud, and she would find him, and likely see him dancing an' all.

The sickness deepened as she made her way towards Burton Street. Why Burton Street she didn't question, but Mulhattan's Hall was in Burton Street and Mrs. McBride was there; he could laugh with Mrs. McBride. And Mrs. Flannagan was there; he would laugh at Mrs. Flannagan and very likely, in spite of his good humour, say rude things to her. If she didn't find him before she got there she would find him in Burton Street.

Five streets away from Mulhattan's Hall she heard him – no one could sing 'Acushla' like her da, drunk or sober.

A group of boys came scampering out of a back lane, one crying to the others, 'Come on. Here's a drunk in Burton Street, he'll make yer split yer sides. Remember? He used to live there – big Mike Shaughnessy.'

She stood against the wall to let them pass; there was no movement from her to defend her right to the pavement now. As she entered Burton Street she saw the boys come to a halt outside a ring of children that surrounded the dancing figure. The street was out, but the grown-ups were keeping to the pavement and their doors and windows.

She did not hurry now – the damage was done. Sorrow, deep and leaden, born of love and humiliation, dragged at her feet. It was the ageless sorrow of a child, old, elemental, welling from depths buried in past eternities, not understood, beyond reason, outbidding its cause, but felt, and felt to be unbearable. Oh Jesus, Mary and Joseph, make him stop. All the people looking at him, and Mrs. Flannagan at her window. Oh blessed, blessed Lord, do something.

'MY FRIEND, HE IS THE FRIEND OF ALL FRIENDS,' Mike was singing now. His head was back and his arms stretched wide and the people listened.

Mary Ann, moving past a group of chuckling women, heard one exclaim, 'He can sing, can Mike. Ah, it's good to have him back, say what you like. What's done this, I wonder? His lady wife left him? I wouldn't be a bit surprised at that an' all.'

A sharp nudge stilled the woman's tongue, and the eyes were turned on Mary Ann. She took no heed but went to the circle in the middle of the road, and slowly pushed herself through the crowd. She was almost within touching distance of Mike when a voice, crying above his, swept over her head and those in the road and turned all eyes towards the Flannagans' upper window. Sarah was leaning out, and what she had called was 'Me da's a grand man!' She was looking triumphantly down on Mary Ann, and behind her, standing back in the shadow, was her mother, with unadulterated satisfaction covering her thin face.

Mike had not seen Mary Ann. He was looking up now to the window, and with an exaggerated Irish twang he cried, 'Oh there you are, me darlin' Mrs. Flannagan – the light of me life.'

Reeling towards the pavement, with the circle giving way to him, he flung up his arms to her, crying, 'Come on down, me darlin', and let me hear the clatter of your refeened twang, for it's that desire alone that has brought me back to me old haunts. And where's me friend Harry? Have you got him tied under the bed?'

The bedroom window closed with a bang, and Mike shouted, stuttering and stammering, 'Ah, don't break me heart. Ah Nellie, come on down, come on woman, and tell me how to get all the heifers on the farm married and made into respectable cows.'

A howl went up from the street, and Mike, appealing to all at large, cried, 'Did you know that? It's the God's own truth as I stand here. Mrs. Flannagan is going to get a bill passed to make every heifer into a decent woman. It'll be a Bull of a Bill, that.'

Mary Ann's trembling lips were shaping the word 'Da' when she was pushed roughly aside by the enraged figure of Mrs. McBride. Mrs. McBride was in her shopping clothes, a black shiny coat and a large black felt hat, lightened here and there with dust and a greenish hue. Grabbing Mike by the arm, she pulled him round, shouting, 'Shut that big mouth of yours and come inside this minute!'

'Here, here! who're you pulling?' Mike's voice became truculent. Then he laughed down on her, 'Aw! Fan. Fat old Fan.' And he attempted to put his arms about her and waltz her around, but Fanny was more than a match for him. She'd had a great deal of training in handling drunks, and before he knew what was happening it was he who was being waltzed round, and in the direction of Mulhattan's Hall. A jerk of her head brought her eldest son from the pavement where he had been enjoying the fun, and Don McBride said pleasantly, 'Come on, away in, Mike, and let's have a crack.'

'Take your hands off me!'

Don took his hands off and retreated, laughing sheepishly, out of harm's way.

'Da! Da! come on.'

Mike's countenance lightened once more, and he exclaimed. 'Why, it's me Mary Ann.' His tone was scoffing as he swayed above her. 'Put me in hell an' me Mary Ann would be there. . . . But you didn't catch up with me, did you?'

He almost fell on her, and she steadied him and took his hand, and guiding him with the forcible assistance of Mrs. McBride from behind she got him up the steep steps and into the house.

Mike was laughing now. Like one child who had got the better of another, he preened himself at Mary Ann.

'I did you, didn't I? O, aye, you thought I'd go to the Long Bar or the Ben Lomond, didn't you? I know! Your da knows all you think! So I beat you. . . . I did a round. But I didn't start where you thought I would. And you know why?'

'No, Da. Lie back, and I'll get you some tea. Can I, Mrs. McBride?'

'Aye, hinny. And I'll give him more than tea,' exclaimed Fanny, busying herself with a number of tins she had taken down from the top shelf of the cupboard.

'Shut up, you old hag, I'm talking to me girl. And you know why, me darlin'?'

'No, Da. Lie back.'

'Well, I'll tell you. . . . 'Cos I knew if I looked into those eyes of yours I'd be done. I couldn't go and get . . . sick, if I looked into those eyes . . . could I now, not real sick? A pint or two, but not real sick. And I'm real sick now, aren't I?'

'Da. Listen.' With her hands on his face Mary Ann tried to rivet his attention.

'Aye, I'm listenin'.' Mike's head rolled on his shoulders. 'I listened to Ratcliffe. I listened to Jonesy. Ratcliffe said to young Len, "You see to Clara," he said. And Jonesy said he heard the old boy say Shaughnessy had to see to Clara ... Shaughnessy may be no good, he won't give his daughter away, but he knows cows. ... He can handle cows, can't he, me darlin'?'

'Yes, Da.... And listen. Listen.'

'I'm listenin'. Ratcliffe knows as much about a farm as me Aunt Fanny. ... That's not you, Fan. Never you, Fan ... aw! never you.' The laughter rumbled thick and deep in his throat and he became launched on a list of Fanny's good points, while Mrs. McBride, pulling Mary Ann to one side, whispered, 'What's happened at all? Has he had a row with the boss?'

'No.'

'Well, what in the name of God is it? He's back where he was.'

The sickness deepened in Mary Ann's breast. As she told her story she glanced at Mike, sprawled now like a giant in the chair. He was rambling again about the farm: Ratcliffe, Len, Jonesy and the cows, but he let slip not the slightest hint about the real reason for his present state. He made no mention of either Lizzie or Bob. That which was eating him up was temporarily buried. His faith in the bottle had not been broken. Once full of liquor, he would be merry ... the trials of life would be dulled, even forgotten – if no one raked them up.

Her eyes cast down, Mary Ann finished the dreaded sentence: 'And he thought me ma was goin' off.'

'The blasted fool!' muttered Fanny. 'And Mr. Quinton goin' to be married. Well, you tell him. Git it into his thick skull whilst I mix him a concoction that'll skite the drink out of him quicker'n the corporation sewer cleaner.'

Mary Ann stood between Mike's legs, her hands on his lapels, and trying to shake his great relaxed body, she said, 'Da ... listen. Will you listen!'

'Aren't I listenin'?'

'No. Stop a minute ... It's about me ma.'

Mike stopped. The good humour faded from his face, his brows drew down and his lips pushed at each other, and with his forearm he went to thrust Mary Ann away, but she hung on to his coat.

'When you listened, Da, it was all wrong what you heard – I want to tell you – listen.'

Mike's eyes became narrow slits of fiery light. In another minute she would not be able to hold him – he would fling her aside and his rage would break. There could be no gentle leading up to the enlightening point. Quickly the words came tumbling out, 'Mr. Quinton's goin' to be married . . . to a girl. He was tellin' me ma.'

Mike's rage did not vanish, but it was checked. And Mary Ann, bringing her imagination to her aid to help penetrate his befuddled state, added hastily, 'She's nice, lovely, an' they're gonna be married in a big church and have it in the papers. Me ma says she is glad, and . . . and,' she added finally, 'she wants you home. Me ma wants you home, Da.'

Mike blinked at her, then looked away to the wall above the cluttered mantelpiece as if he expected to find there, written large, words that would further bear out this news . . . this disturbing news that was going to make him look a fool, for that's what he would be, his reeling brain told him, if this were true. And he was no fool. No, by God! he was not. With a great show of effort, he was making to rise from the chair when Fanny checked him.

'Here! Get this down you.'

'What's it, eh? Poison?'

'Aye . . . get it down you.'

'Fan,' he took the cup from her, 'do you know . . . what . . . the child's tellin' me?'

'I know well enough. Drink up!'

'Now listen . . . listen. I'm no fool, I've been duped afore. Once bitten.'

'Drink!' The order would have done credit to a sergeant-major.

Mike drank, throwing the contents of the cup against the back of his throat at one go, and in the next instant the cup was flung across the room and he was out of the chair, coughing and gasping. And between the gasps he spluttered, 'In . . . in the name of God! . . .'

'Ah, it won't kill you.'

'M ... m ... m ... my God ... Fan!'

'Ah, be quiet, will you!'

Coughing as though his lungs were burning, he leant over the high back of the armchair, his mouth wide open.

'Come on ... get your head under the tap and you'll be nearly yourself again. And stop making such a to-do. That was me old man's tonic. It's a corpse reviver, if ever there was one. The quick an' the dead, he called it. You had to be quick if you didn't want to be dead. Come on, now, under the tap.'

Half leading, half pushing him, she got him into the scullery, and, pointing to the sink, said, 'Get your head down.'

Shaken into temporariy docility by her command, Mike obeyed Fanny and put his head under the tap.

Standing now close to the sink, her eyes unblinking, Mary Ann watched his every movement with patient concern, and when finally he lifted his dripping head and almost fell on his face, she steadied him, stiffening her tiny weight to check his fall. Then she led him into the kitchen once again and to his chair. Standing on a stool, she helped him to dry his head. When this was completed Fanny surveyed him. 'You're a blasted fool!' she said.

'Shut up!'

'I'll not shut up. Have you any money left?'

'Why?'

'If you have, I'd sport a taxi.'

'Taxi, be damned!' Mike got to his feet. 'I'll be all right.'

He stood swaying a little; but he no longer reeled. As yet he was not sober enough to feel shame-faced, but he was sober enough not to want to walk the street again.

Fanny, sensing this, said, 'Go on out the back way with you then. ... And look, put this dry muffler round your neck.'

Mary Ann said no word of thanks. She only looked at the old woman who was looking at Mike as he slowly tucked the muffler into his braces. And when Fanny turned and nodded encouragingly to her, Mary Ann, incapable of using her voice in any way because of the lump that was blocking her windpipe, followed the shambling figure of her father into the backyard. Without having to turn, Mary Ann knew that Mrs. McBride was following their progress up the lane, and she knew that her head would be shaking. For some reason this increased the size of the lump still further.

She led Mike through all the side ways she knew towards the bus stop, and they met no one who took any notice of them until they turned the corner of Delius Street, and there on the opposite side of the road and coming towards them, was Father Owen. His long length bent against the wind, he was holding on to his hat, and at the sight of him, Mary Ann's heart gave a painful leap. Father Owen was the last person in the world she wished to meet at this moment. Father Owen thought her da a grand man; he didn't know he drank; hadn't he sworn when he was standing beneath the cross that he knew her da never touched a drop? Even if her da only looked . . . a little sick now, Father Owen mustn't see him.

Being unable to work it out, but feeling that for the priest's own peace of mind he must not find himself to have been mistaken, she suddenly pulled at Mike's arm and, turning him about, guided him round the corner and steered him up Delius Street's back lane. Had she kept straight on it is possible that Father Owen would have passed without noticing them, but the scurry she made and Mike's protesting arm flung wide attracted the priest's attention. Father Owen had no need to question who they were, Mike could never hope to disguise himself, and Mary Ann . . . well, back view or front view there was only one Mary Ann.

His face took on a sadness and he slowed his pace to allow her sufficient time to make the desired get-away with her burden – her cross, he thought, her beloved cross. He, too, shook his head.

Breathing now more easily, Mary Ann neared the bus stop. Soon they would be home and her da would be in bed, and nobody would have seen him. The crowds in Burton Street did not matter now, they belonged to a past world that had no connection with the farm.

The bus came, and Mike, pushing her before him, hoisted himself on board, and since the only empty seats were at the far end of the bus they made their way towards these and sat down, right opposite Lena and Mrs. Ratcliffe!

After staring for a moment at the wife of his boss, Mike ran his tongue over his lips, and, ironically, he laughed to himself. His mind was clear enough to make him realize that there was no hope of disguising his condition, so with exaggerated bravado he doffed his cap and exclaimed loudly, 'Good day to you, Mrs. Ratcliffe.'

Mary Ann prayed swiftly that the Ratcliffes might be struck blind and, incidentally, deaf; that some act of God might waft them out of the bus and drop them in the road somewhere; and at last, in desperation, she prayed that the bus might collide with something and that they would all be killed.

God did not apparently hear any of her prayers, or if He did, He chose to ignore them. And after a journey during which her agony was, she knew, only a foretaste of that which was to come, they reached the cross-roads. After alighting, by some strange manoeuvre the Ratcliffes managed to walk down the lane behind them. And to Mary Ann's bewilderment, her da's swaying became worse. Then came the final humiliation, he raised his voice in song.

'Listen to me.' Stooping quietly and swiftly, Lizzie dragged Michael up from the fender where he sat slumped. Her handling of him was rough and her whispering fierce. 'It was a mistake, I tell you; it won't happen again.'

She stared at him, forcing him to believe her, but his eyes dropped from hers and his head sank, and he muttered, 'It will, it's Mulhattan's Hall all over again.'

'It isn't . . . He didn't mean to do it . . . It was my fault.'

Michael looked quickly up at her. And Lizzie, drawing in her breath, said haltingly, 'It was something that . . . that happened.'

It was impossible to explain to this son of hers exactly what had happened. Mary Ann could witness the intricacies, the pitfalls, and the tightrope walkings of marriage, and even handle them, but not Michael. His father's weakness found only two reactions in him, depression and anger – and now the anger was to the fore.

Pulling himself from her hands, he cried, 'He's spoilt everything, as he always does. The whole place knows . . .

Singing in the lane! And bringing the Joneses out. And Mrs. Ratcliffe there.'

'Stop shouting, our Michael, you'll wake him.' Mary Ann, who had been standing aside watching her mother fighting to keep Michael's respect for the man who was now snoring upstairs, pushed at her brother with doubled fists and hissed, 'Shut up! It's like me ma says, he won't do it again.'

'Aw, you!' Michael rounded on her fiercely. 'You'd always stick up for him, you like to see him drunk.'

'Oh . . . h!' The injustice of this remark left her for the moment verbally dry, but the 'Oh . . . h!' expressed her hurt, and Michael, more quiet now, said again, 'Well, you always stick up for him.'

'Be quiet!' said Lizzie tersely. 'Here's Len coming across the yard.' She stood watching the farmhand approach, and when he neared the window she went and opened the back door.

Looking somewhat sheepish, the young fellow said, 'Is Mike in, Mrs. Shaughnessy?'

Lizzie did not immediately answer him – the whole farm community knew Mike was in – but then she said flatly, 'Yes, he's in.'

'It's . . . it's the boss. He wants him in the byres. He says he wants him to see to Clara.'

Lizzie's eyes became cold. 'It's his half day.'

'I know, Mrs. Shaughnessy.' The young man's tone was genuinely apologetic. 'It isn't me. I was quite willing to see to her, but them's his orders.'

Lizzie's expression did not alter. 'Very well,' she said, 'I'll tell him.'

She closed the door and walked into the kitchen, where both Michael's and Mary Ann's eyes asked her the same question. She did not answer them.

Mary Ann stood listening to her mother ascending the stairs, and putting her thumb into the side of her mouth, she started systematically to bite hard round the nail. Her da had only been upstairs for half an hour, and she'd had a job getting him up, for he would sing and laugh, and he hadn't spoken to her ma, nor her ma to him – their talking would come later, she knew, when he was sober. And now she was going to waken him, and he'd still be . . . a bit sick. Not even

97

in the most secret places of her mind did she imprint the word drunk. She heard him snort loudly, then shout something. Then there was silence. Presently her mother came downstairs, and a few minutes later Mike followed, and to Mary Ann's deepening distress she saw he was in a bad mood, like he used to be after he had sobered up in the mornings. Only now he wasn't sober, not really sober. His face was heavy with sleep and his eyes angry. He passed his hands through his matted hair, then said to Mary Ann, 'Fetch me boots.'

Quickly Mary Ann brought the boots. He took them from her, but looked at Lizzie where she was standing with her back to him staring into the fire. His voice deep in his throat and still fuddled, he said, 'You see the plan of campaign, don't you? Ratcliffe's got a line at last. With me very own hands I've given him a line. I'm to look after a sick cow, a valuable sick cow, and I'm in no condition to see to even a mountain goat. He's hoping, is Ratcliffe.'

Lizzie said nothing, but continued to stare into the fire. And as Mike pulled savagely on his laces, he went on, speaking as if to himself, 'Jonesy heard the old man leave orders for me to see to her this morning; but Ratcliffe wasn't letting the old boy give him any orders, so Len was detailed. But now that his lady wife has informed him I am drunk he sees his chance. Well' – Mike knotted the laces and gritted his teeth – 'I'll show him. Drunk or sober, I'll show him I could buy and sell him where a cow's concerned. Where's me coat?'

'Here, Da.'

Mary Ann, the coat already on her arm, handed it to him. Thrusting his arms into it, Mike noticed Michael for the first time. He stared at the boy, then pulling his cap from his pocket he pressed it on to his head, saying fiercely, 'And don't look at me like that or I'll wring your blasted ear for you.'

The door banged behind him, and Mary Ann, moving slowly to the window, watched him cross the yard, his step still uncertain.

CHAPTER EIGHT

THE LOFT

MIKE leaned against the stanchion of the sick bay and wiped the running sweat from his face with his forearm. There was no sound, not even a secretive night sound to bring comfort. There was only the heavy, sweet warm smell pressing down on him, and the dead cow and calf lying at his feet. He gazed pityingly down on the animals. Clara had been so human, she had fought to the last. After seeming to hold the calf for an unnecessarily long time, she had struggled valiantly to bring it, but to no purpose. It was just after twelve when she turned her head and looked at him and made a sound, a quite uncowlike sound. Remembering it now, he thought, she knew she couldn't bring it off.

He looked at his watch. It was a quarter past three. He felt as tired as though he had done a double shift in the shipyard. He moved out of the bay and sat down on a low box and leant his head against the byre. He'd have to go and tell Ratcliffe, and there'd be hell to pay. Without a doubt, he'd push the blame on to him. In the back of his now sober but sleep-hazy mind, he vaguely sensed Ratcliffe's plan. . . . A man couldn't be sacked for being drunk off the job, but he could be sacked for what he did, or didn't do, when drunk on the job. Ratcliffe had been in three times during the evening, the last time just before twelve o'clock. However fuddled he may have appeared earlier on, Ratcliffe could certainly not deny that he was sober then, for they had spoken together quite ordinarily; and Ratcliffe had suggested that Clara would hang on for at least another twelve hours.

Well, Clara was dead, and besides Ratcliffe's reactions, the old man would go sky high. She had been his best cow. He had paid a great deal of money for her, hoping to start a stock.

Mike rasped his chin with his hand, then pressed his eyeballs. He was dead beat, and he would no sooner get into bed than he would have to get up again. His mind swung to Lizzie, and he moved restlessly. He had her to face, too, and explain yet once again why he had been a blasted weak fool. Other fellows could get knocks and stand up to them, but he always had to seek consolation. But when the knock hadn't been a knock at all, only the result of the fermentation in his mind, the explanation was going to be harder than ever before.

Well, that was one scene that could be put off. He would sleep here, and then he'd be in better shape to face her in the morning. He'd go now and get this business over with Ratcliffe before turning in on the straw.

The arrangement settled in his mind, he sat on, and the warm quietness settled upon him like a blanket.

Mike was brought sharply from the far depths of sleep by a blow in the middle of his back. There is no mistaking a heavy-booted foot, and the fact that he had been kicked brought him out of the straw and to his feet as if he had been suddenly stung into life. He looked a ferocious and forbidding sight, his hair with the straw in it standing up on end and his arm drawn back ready to strike.

'What the hell d'you think you're doin'?' he yelled.

Ratcliffe, his face grim and his voice cutting in its meaning, said, 'And what the hell do you think you're doing? Look at that!' He swung round and pointed to the dead animals. 'Gone; both of them, while you lie snoring your head off.'

Mike's arm had dropped, but his voice was still menacing: 'Don't be a blasted fool . . .!'

'What!' Ratcliffe roared. 'You remember who you're talking to.'

'I know who I'm talking to all right. I did me utmost, but I could save neither of them. The calf was strangled afore it came, you can see that.'

'Why didn't you come for me?'

'How could I, I couldn't leave her? If you had done the right thing you would have left the lad with me.'

'Don't you tell me what I should do. But if I had let the lad see to her I'd have had a live cow and calf this morning

They wouldn't have died time he was sleeping his drink off.'

The two men glared at each other. The dislike, born at their first meeting and fostered on Ratcliffe's part by his wife, now flared into open hatred. His brows drawn down and his lips thrust out, Mike growled, 'So that's your game. I knew it. I got drunk yesterday and gave you the chance you've been waiting for. Clara being sick just fitted in, didn't it? When I was sober you wouldn't let me near her, although you had your orders from the old man. Aye, I know all about that, an' all.'

'I'm in charge of this farm and I'll put my men where I like.'

'Well, here's one you won't put where you like.'

'Won't I? We'll see . . . you're fired!'

'Da! Da!' The cry cut through their shouting and caused them both to swing round to where Mary Ann stood hugging a coat about her. Her face was chalk coloured and her brown eyes looked like great black sloes, and, as such, incapable of blinking. Her gaze was not fixed on Mike but on Mr. Ratcliffe, as if, instead of his flesh and blood, she saw him embodied in the fiery tissues of the devil himself.

Even when Mike rapped out, 'What you doin' here? get yourself back home,' she still did not lift her gaze from Ratcliffe, who, finding the intensity of her eyes more unnerving than any expression of Mike's, swung round, saying over his shoulder as he marched away, 'Come to the office at nine tomorrow morning.'

'Be damned to you!' cried Mike, stepping forward.

'Da, oh Da! don't.' Mary Ann was now tugging at Mike's hand. 'Be quiet, Da . . . Oh, Da!'

'You be quiet and get yourself home to bed.' Mike made to thrust her away, then stopped. The sight of her face, so pinched with fear, and her eyes so weighed with sadness, checked his harshness, for he saw in her expression all the unhappiness that was about to descend on them again, and as usual through him. Yet the blame was not entirely his. Ratcliffe had meant to get rid of him; it had to come sooner or later.

'Oh, Da . . . Da.'

'It's all right. Be quiet now,' he said roughly.

His anger was seeping from him and he put his hand gently on her head. 'Why did you come out at this time of the morning, and it still dark? What if your mother finds you gone?'

'I couldn't sleep, Da, and I went to the landing window to see if the light was still on here. And it was. And I had to come.... Will you come to bed now, Da?'

'No. No, I can't. Anyway it's near time to get up, and I've got some work to do.'

Although his eyes did not turn towards the byre, Mary Ann's gaze slid fearfully round. Before he could move in front of her to block her view she had seen Clara and the calf.

Even to her child's eyes the animals did not look merely asleep, their relaxation was too complete. She took several shuddering breaths, then, turning swiftly to Mike, she buried her face in his thigh and bit on his trousers to still her crying.

'There now, there now.' He lifted her into his arms. 'They're all right, they're just fast asleep. They've gone to. ...' He found it difficult to use the jargon that was as natural to her as breathing, but finally he brought out ... 'heaven.' But it brought no comfort; her crying mounted. So pulling his coat off a peg, he put it round his shoulders and about her, and made his way in the bleak dawn towards the cottage. As he went, strangely enough, it wasn't the coming meeting with Lizzie he thought of, or yet that with Ratcliffe or the old man, but he thought of Mrs. McMullen and how she would gloat over this latest development, which would prove conclusively that he wasn't any good. And in his own mind, for the first time, drunk or sober, he was agreeing with her.

At twenty past nine on the same Sunday morning Mary Ann was waiting for the bus to take her into Jarrow and to Mass. She had refused to be persuaded to go to Mass in Felling with Michael, although Felling was much nearer to the farm. Now she was wondering whether, if she attended the grown-up Mass at eleven o'clock, Miss Thompson would consider it the same as her going to the Children's

Mass. Miss Thompson might not even miss her presence at the ten o'clock Mass; but Sarah Flannagan would, and she would find some way to suggest to the teacher that she hadn't been to Mass at all. With a slight movement of her head, she dismissed the consequences of her premeditated action, for this worry was infinitesimal compared with the grief now loading her mind. Sarah Flannagan and Miss Thompson were irritants that, given time, she could deal with, but there was no time to deal with this other thing.

In the freshly budding flecked green of the hawthorn hedge flanking the opposite side of the road she saw her mother's face as it had looked a few minutes earlier when she left the house. It bore the old look of Mulhattan's Hall again. And yet her ma and da hadn't fought.

Her mother's attitude had been disturbing. The quiet way she had taken Mike's report of the scene with Ratcliffe; the sadness and pity in her face as she had looked at him created an odd effect in Mary Ann. It had increased instead of diminished her fear of the future, for although her ma had said, 'Well, there are other jobs,' there had been a hopelessness about her. Like the return of a dread disease, once imagined gone for ever, it seemed now useless to fight against the sentence it imposed, even though her mother herself had seemed to grasp at hope when she said, 'Why don't you go to Mr. Lord and tell him everything?'

'Go to him? Not likely,' Mike had said. 'I'm crawling to no man. And what would be the good anyway; won't Ratcliffe phone him as soon as he's out of bed?'

What time did Mr. Lord get out of bed? It was Sunday morning and likely he'd be having a lie in. Mary Ann prayed fervently that this would be so. This morning of all mornings she prayed that sleep would lie heavily on the old man, that the bed would drag and that if Ben came to call him he would growl at him and turn over.

She sent up these urgent requests while she gazed steadfastly down on her prayer book held tightly between her two hands, as if her prayer, being filtered through this passport to heaven, would reach the celestial quarters so coated with piety that a refusal on the part of the Holy Family to grant her desires would be practically impossible. Already she had a plan of campaign mapped out . . . roughly sketched would be more accurate. She would go to Mr. Lord and get the first one in. If she could get her say in before Mr. Ratcliffe, all would -- she imagined -- be well. Not about Clara. No, that was something beyond her province. In any case, although sorrow for Clara's fate was still touching her, it bore no comparison with the sorrow for the fate that awaited her da should Mr. Lord hear he had been drunk yesterday. It was this and this alone she must work on; she must in some way convince him that her da had been solid and sober when he went to the cowshed. . . . But how?

The how did not unduly worry her either. It was a long way in the bus to Mr. Lord's . . . two miles. By then she would have thought of something.

As always when Mary Ann left her subconscious to deal with her difficulties it never failed her. She was sitting in the bus looking disconsolately out of the window when her eyes saw a poster depicting a number of startling scenes from *The Robe* . . . There she had the solution. She would tell him her da had taken her to see that picture. She had studied this poster before, for there was one on her way to school, and she had been fascinated by the physique of the two men and the beauty of the lady, but mostly she had been touched by the three crosses on the hill and . . . the poor Lord, hanging there.

But not until she had left the bus and was half-way up the drive was her enthusiasm for her plan dampened and her courage halved, for she remembered, literally with a start that brought her to a stop, that the feeling between Mr. Lord and herself was not as it had once been. The Lord she was going to now was as formidable as the man into whose house she had gate-crashed a few months previously. Now her steps were slow and she approached the door with the same trepidation she had experienced on that first visit.

Ben answered her ring, and she looked up into his wizened face and said 'Hallo' with unusual humility. To her surprise he didn't growl at her and say, 'What d'you want?' but stood aside to let her in. And she was forced for the moment to take her mind off Mr. Lord and look at his servant, for he was not scowling at her. It was a very strange and surprising thing to see, but in his eyes there was a look of kindness. He almost looked as if he were glad to see her, which placed him immediately in the category of an ally. Her glance moved away across the large dim hall towards the dining-room, then back again. And she strained up to him and whispered 'Is he all right?'

Ben moved his head slowly from side to side, and Mary Ann's mouth formed a soundless 'Oh', while she watched with widening eyes Ben's creaking length being bent towards her. And when his parchment-skin face was on a level with her own, she was so taken aback by his cordiality that she could scarcely take in the dread import of what he was saying.

'Mr. Ratcliffe's phoned about the cow, and the master is' – Ben paused before adding – 'very annoyed' as if he found the expression inadequate to describe his master's reaction.

Mary Ann dragged her gaze from the interesting spectacle of Ben's face at close quarters and looked down at her thumb, then conveyed it to her mouth and nibbled at the nail. That Mr. Ratcliffe was a nasty rotten beast, he was. She wished he would drop down dead, she did. Yet hope, never utterly dead in her, prompted the thought that although Mr. Ratcliffe had phoned about Clara he may not have mentioned her da and yesterday. There was a possibility that she had still time to prove to Mr. Lord that her da couldn't have been sick yesterday.

After a pathetic glance in Ben's direction she went slowly towards the dining-room door, tapped once, and, without waiting for an answer, opened it and went in.

It was at once evident to her that Mr. Lord was not surprised to see her. He was sitting by the fire filling his pipe. She saw from the table that he had just finished his breakfast. His head moved a little and his eyes slid towards her, but without resting on her or seeming to take in her presence. Then they returned to his pipe, and he went on filling it, pushing the tobacco into the bowl with gentle pressures that misled Mary Ann and made her think: He's not really mad or else he'd be poking it in.

'Hallo,' she said.

There was no return greeting to this, but she moved closer – she was used to him being grumpy. 'I'm going to Mass. I was on me way and I thought . . .' She paused. This was too much like real lying. She had been about to add, 'I thought

I'd look in and see you.' She knew that only the present emergency had brought her here, yet there was something she was unable to explain to herself, for she was glad to be here, glad to see him. She was experiencing a similar feeling to that which she had when she played houses and wrapped her doll up against the cold and nursed it on her knee by the fire. Bertha roused her pity by the coldness of its china body; this old man by his loneliness, visible to her even through the layers of his severity. She wanted to put her hand on his and say something funny – daft funny, to make him laugh.

'Well what do you want; you want something, don't you?'

This direct attack nonplussed her for the moment, and she said, 'Yes ... no ... yes. I mean—' She stopped. She could see now that he was in a bad temper ... he was in a flaming temper. And like her da he was worse when he was quiet, and more unmanageable. If he would bawl at her she would know what to do.

Mr. Lord stopped pushing at his pipe, and he looked at her with a look that sent hope fleeing from her. Then he said, 'You have come to tell me that the cow isn't dead, nor her calf. The calf is alive and kicking, isn't it? And you have come to tell me' – his neck moved out of his collar, and his head with small jerks emphasized each word – 'that your father was not drunk yesterday.'

She stared back at him. Tragedy filled the space between them, the tragedy of her da getting the sack, of her ma packing up their things.

'He was drunk yesterday, wasn't he?' Mr. Lord seemed to derive some satisfaction in repeating this statement, for it was accompanied by a sneer, which reminded her of Sarah Flannagan when she said, 'Aw, you! You see, I told you so.' Mostly from habit, the denial slipped from her lips: 'He wasn't.'

'What!'

The force of the word, which owed nothing to loudness but everything to its intensity, sent her back from him. He heaved himself out of the chair. 'Why do I listen to you? Get yourself away!'

He spoke to her, not as to a child, but as to an adult, an equal, for that was how he thought of her. Had she appeared to him merely as a child, he would have lost interest in her after their first encounter. But from the first he had recognized in her an adult quality, a similar quality to one which he himself possessed and which centred around his tenacity. No one of his experience had fought for what he wanted against heavy odds as he had done, and as she was continually doing. Yet this knowledge at the same time irked him, for with this very trait she would grow up defending that waster. All her efforts and thoughts would be centred around him, and she would emerge into womanhood like millions of other women, ordinary, except for the doubtful quality of a father fixation. Whereas, had she received the proper schooling to train her nimble mind there was, he imagined, no limit to the height she could eventually reach ... away from Mike's influence, and himself behind her. He turned to the window. He would not allow himself to follow up this thought, or look at her while she spoke.

'I'm going, and whoever told you that's a liar. ... Mr. Ratcliffe's a liar, I know he is. He wouldn't let me da look after Clara. He put Len on, and I heard you tell him to let me da do it.'

She knew she had caught his attention with this last piece of news, for she saw his head lift. She went on, nodding at his back, 'Mr. Ratcliffe's got it in for me da; he always has. He gives him the worst jobs. Mr. Jones says if it was him he would have left. And me ma's wanted me da to mention it to you but he wouldn't. And Mr. Ratcliffe only sent for me da last night out of spite because ...' Her flow ceased, and Mr. Lord turned from the window and finished the sentence for her, '... Because he knew your father was drunk. That's it, isn't it?'

'He wasn't' – now her chin was jerking up at him – 'he was solid and sober!'

'Stop that!' Mr. Lord's voice had risen. And hers went to an even higher key as she replied with heat, 'I won't! ... he wasn't ... he took me out, he did, and we went into Jarrow.'

'And he got drunk.'

'He didn't, I tell you!'

'I don't want any of your shouting.'

'I'm not shouting. You'll believe nothing, nothing at all.

He didn't get drunk, so there, 'cos he couldn't, we went to the pictures. You can ask anybody.'

'Who's anybody?' It sounded now as if he wanted to believe her.

'Mrs. McBride ... and ... and ...' Her mind rushed madly around, searching for another likely defender ... and found one ... 'and Father Owen,' she added. 'He knows we went. "Enjoy the picture, Mary Ann," he said, " 'cos it's about Jesus." '

Eeh! She stood petrified at the length her imagination had stretched, and also at what it was achieving, for Mr. Lord's brows were drawn together in a decided question.

'You saw Father Owen?'

'Yes.' It was a very small yes.

'And he knew you were going to the pictures with your father?'

'... Yes.'

The bushy brows were drawn over the eyes. 'What did you see at the pictures?'

'The Robe.'

'The Robe?'

'Yes.'

'What was it about?'

'About two men and a beautiful lady.'

'Yes?'

'And ... and Our Lord being crucified.'

'Go on.'

'And ... and ... ' She stared fixedly at him, trying to conjure up the poster again. But it would not be brought up, and all she had to defend her cause now was her knowledge of Bible history, and she had never liked Bible history, for she had never been any good at it. 'And Peter and the cock crowing three times,' she said haltingly. 'And Our Lord giving everybody fish and bread and saying, if there's anybody here who hasn't told a lie he can do the pelting. It was a nice picture.' Her voice trailed off.

The silence pressed down on the room, and it told her more plainly than any words that she had failed. He had likely seen the picture.

When he turned from her she stood for a while longer. Then taking heed of the rising lump in her throat she swung round and ran out of the room and into the hall, where her swift entry startled Ben in his eavesdropping. Still running, she dashed through the doorway and down the drive. . . .

It was nearly one o'clock when she returned home. Mass had brought no comfort. Being the grown-ups' Mass, Father Owen had been inaccessible. The Holy Family too had offered not the slightest solace; they had stared back at her as if they couldn't care less. And now, it seemed unbelievable but it was true, there was her grannie sitting at the table with her hat off, and from the expression on her face, Mary Ann judged that she already knew everything. Her grannie, she had always known, was like the devil – she received first-hand information about the bad things. But it would now seem that she was quicker than the devil.

'Hallo . . . you been to Mass?'

Mrs. McMullen's tone was civil, which in itself was a bad sign.

'Yes.' Mary Ann turned to her mother. 'Ma, where's me . . .'

Lizzie cut short her inquiry: 'Get your things off,' she said.

'Which Mass were you at?' asked Mrs. McMullen.

'The eleven o'clock.'

'Why didn't you go to the ten, that's your Mass, isn't it?'

'Yes.'

'Then why didn't you go?'

' 'Cos I didn't want to!' The shouted words startled both Mrs. McMullen and Lizzie, but before Lizzie could remonstrate with her daughter, Mrs. McMullen's hand came across Mary Ann's ear in a resounding slap.

Lizzie caught her as she reeled back and held her tightly, and looking straight at her mother, she said, quietly, 'Don't do that again, I'm telling you.'

'Then teach her some manners . . . Shouting at me. And after asking her a civil question. . . . It's like him, she is, uncivilized, bringing trouble wherever she goes.'

'That's enough,' said Lizzie. She pushed Mary Ann from her.

'It isn't enough. I've prophesied this time and again. I've been waiting for it.'

'Then you're not disappointed,' said Lizzie.

'No, I'm not. And neither was the whole of Burton Street. Mrs. Flannagan said it was the peak of his career, the way he went on yesterday. He made a holy show of himself. The whole of Jarrow was out.'

'It wasn't. Shut up, you!' Mary Ann's face, except where her grandmother's fingers had left their imprint, was white. 'Shut up! You're . . . you're a cheeky bitch. You are! . . . you are!'

Lifting Mary Ann bodily, Lizzie carried her from the room and up the stairs. There was the sound of a door banging overhead, followed by loud sobbing; then Lizzie came slowly back into the kitchen.

Mrs. McMullen was standing now, her hat perched on one hand, while with the other she pulled the velvet bow into shape. Lizzie stood just inside the door. Her face wore the protecting tightness bred of past encounters with her mother.

'What,' she asked quietly, 'do you hope to gain from it?'

'What do you mean? . . . Go on . . . go on and put the blame on me for her being like a gutter-snipe.'

'If,' went on Lizzie, ignoring her mother's side-tracking, 'I was to do what you want and leave him, and suppose I couldn't earn enough myself to keep us like you imagine we should be kept, who would you have me turn to now that Bob is going to be married?' And having sprung this piece of news, she waited.

Mrs. McMullen's hands remained poised over her hat. The news was evidently a shock to her, for her prim features were sagging with surprise as she brought out, 'Bob! . . . I don't believe it. He wouldn't.'

'He told me himself yesterday.'

'I don't believe it, not a word. There's only ever been you.'

'He is marrying a girl from Jesmond. Pringle's daughter . . . the fruit people.'

Mrs. McMullen sat down. The muscles of her face were tight again. 'The turncoat,' she muttered. 'He wouldn't dare come and tell me. Why, he said only afore Christmas that the greatest pleasure he'd get from building the old man's house would be that he could see you.' She turned her small sharp eyes on to her daughter. 'It's a broken heart he's doing it out of . . . that's what it is.'

'You can stop deluding yourself on that point too,' said Lizzie. 'I happen to know she is young and very lovely. And what is more, she'll be quite rich one day.'

Mrs. McMullen seemed unable to find an answer to this. She sat for a while longer in silence; then rising, she pulled on her hat without the fuss she usually accorded this operation, grabbed her coat from a hook on the door, and for the very first time in her life left her daughter without a word of admonition.

After her mother's departure, Lizzie sat down, and resting her elbows on the table and her head in her hands, she said with utter weariness, 'Dear God. Dear God.'

On Monday morning Mary Ann said she was feeling bad.

'Where?' asked her mother. 'Have you a pain?'

'No,' said Mary Ann. 'I'm just sick.'

This was true enough; she was feeling sick, the sickness born of anxiety. But she had experienced this before, and it hadn't prevented her from getting up and going to school. This morning, however, she didn't want to go to school; it was as urgent as a matter of life and death that she should be here when Mr. Ratcliffe sacked her da, as he would do at nine o'clock.

Lizzie wasn't fooled, but her mind, dwelling on the same thing as Mary Ann's, was too harassed to cope with her daughter. She could only say, 'Well, you'll go at dinner time, mind.'

'Yes, Ma.'

The victory had been easy. She lay, not curled up as she usually did when she was enjoying a lie in, but with her short length stretched tautly out. Soon Michael would come up for his schoolbag and things, then she would get up and go to the farm.

She turned her head and stared at the wall. On her eye level were three humpty elephants following a giraffe, a tiger and a penguin. Her da had pasted the animals all round her corner. He had cut them out of a book especially for her. And now she would have to leave them; some other girl would have this corner. She stared at the ceiling. Where would they go to live? They couldn't go back to Mulhattan's Hall because the attics had been taken. Perhaps Mrs. McBride would take them in. . . . But she had only two rooms.

Her da had offered no opinion as to what was going to happen to them. He had been quiet; he hadn't opened his mouth all day yesterday, nor had he eaten anything, not a bit of dinner, nor yet supper. But twice he had made himself some tea, thick black tea.

'You're not sick.'

Michael's appearance from behind the curtain and his accusation startled her, and she stammered, 'I . . . I . . . I am.'

'You're not . . . you only want to nose around.'

They continued to stare hostilely at each other. Then Michael, turning away to close the door stealthily, came back to her bed and, sitting on it, said, 'Listen. If you want to hear anything go up in the loft.'

'But who'll I hear there?' Mary Ann was sitting up now.

'Mr. Ratcliffe. . . . Look, listen to what I'm saying. You know the long loft where the feed's kept. Well, the end of it runs over the dairy, doesn't it?'

'Yes.' Mary Ann was not certain.

'Well, next to the dairy is the store Mr. Ratcliffe turned into an office, isn't it?'

'Yes.' She was still not certain, for the topographical situation as Michael explained it was not clear to her.

'Well, get up in the loft. Go behind the bales until you come to where there's just the beams, and if you lie along the end one, nearest to the back of the loft, you can hear them talking down below.'

'Who?'

'Well, anybody who's there. And Mr. Lord'll be there. And Mr. Ratcliffe'll be telling him the tale, and you can see if he tells him the truth.'

Their faces were close together, and she saw from the troubled hurt look in his eyes that in his own way Michael was as concerned for their da as she was. But she couldn't as yet see what good it was going to do listening to Mr. Ratcliffe talking to Mr. Lord, and she said so.

'It'll be no use if I do hear.'

'It will. Me da can go and deny it.'

'He won't.'

'He will if me ma puts her foot down.'

The idea of her da being forced to defend himself under the pressure of a foot being put down, whether her ma's or anybody else's, was enough to make her obstinate. 'I'm not going to listen,' she said.

Michael sprang up from the bed, his face almost as red as his hair. 'Oh you . . . You little . . .!'

'I'm not.' Mary Ann denied her sub-title before it was uttered. 'If me ma makes me da do something, they'll row, and then things'll be just as bad.'

'Nothing can be as bad as him being out of work and likely having to go back to the yards.'

They stared at each other for a moment longer. Then Michael turned away, collected his bag from behind the curtain and went downstairs. When she heard the outer door bang, she got up and dressed hurriedly; but her descent of the stairs was slow, as befitted a sick person.

Lizzie, clearing the table, said, 'Can you eat anything?'

'No,' said Mary Ann.

And this was true, too, for she had no appetite. She fiddled about with her hair ribbon. She sat down. She stood up. She opened a picture book and turned the pages without seeing anything. Then she asked quietly, 'Can I go out for a walk, Ma?'

'Yes,' said Elizabeth.

That was all. She did not question whither the walk would take her; she knew. She did not say, 'If you are sick, you had better stay in,' for she also knew that that would aggravate the particular kind of sickness.

Immediately she reached the lane, Mary Ann started to run. She did not turn into the main road which would lead her to the farmyard, but cut across a field that would bring her to the back of the barn. Through a knot-hole in the barn she saw her da. He was cleaning a machine, rubbing it with an oily rag. He was working slowly as if he was tired. She saw Mr. Jones come in and heard him ask, 'We gonner start on the binder, Mike?' and her da reply, 'Might as well.'

From the time she saw Mike and Mr. Jones move into the far dimness of the barn until she climbed the ladder to the loft was only a matter of seconds, for she knew that if she was spotted by her da she would be ordered home.

The loft was warm and had a stingy smell that made her want to sneeze, and it was not a little frightening, for it seemed bigger than usual and the stacked bales higher. Cautiously she followed Michael's instructions, until she came to the beams naked of floor-boards. There were only four of them and they could not have measured more than three feet before they disappeared into the slope of the roof, but to Mary Ann they appeared to be yards long. She stretched cautiously over them and looked down. It was dark, and she could make out nothing. When tentatively she put her hand down in between the beams, it touched the roughness of bricks, and she could not tell what was actually beneath her, but Michael had said if she lay across the last beam she would be able to hear. Trembling, she attempted the feat.

A man, or even a boy, could have rested easily over the beams, but her slight body would have fallen in between them, and as her courage was not of the kind that could perform physical feats, it took a great deal more of it to lie along a beam than it would have taken to swear her own life away.

After easing herself back and forwards a number of times for practice she sat and waited for voices to come to her. The minutes took on the length of hours, and the only sound that she heard was the distant closing of a door. It was strange but there weren't even any farm sounds here. The bales made the corner a silent world in which she could hear only her own breathing, and she didn't like the sound of that. It was like being all alone in the lane on a dark night. . . . And then she heard a voice . . . or the echo of one. It came as if from the bottom of a well. In a second she was lying along the beam. Now the voice was joined by another; but it wasn't her da's, it was Mr. Lord's. But what was he saying, she couldn't make out a thing?

The urgency of the situation overcoming her fear, she thrust her head down between the beams, and, like the voices on the old records Mrs. McBride used to play on her gramophone, she heard them talking. They came quietly at first, then rose swiftly.

'You didn't carry out my instructions.'

'Am I managing this farm or not?'

'You are managing it, but what you seem to forget is that you don't own it. I told you to let Shaughnessy see to her.'

'He's not capable.'

'There you know you are wrong. Whatever else he lacks it's not a knowledge of animals. Remember Douglas's bull. It was he who warned you against buying it. Isn't that so?'

'The bull was all right. . . . We are not talking about the bull but about the cow.'

'Why did you send for him on Saturday night after putting Morley on?'

'Because Morley wanted a break.'

'He didn't. You sent for Shaughnessy because you knew he was drunk. You were to ring for the vet if the animal got worse, but what did you do? You wanted a handle, didn't you?'

'Look here, Mr. Lord, you want to be careful.'

'You wanted to get rid of him.'

'I didn't.'

'All right, then, why do you say you mean to sack him?'

'Because he neglected his work.'

'What if I say he didn't neglect his work, and he stays on?'

'You won't.'

'Won't I?'

'No . . . because if you do I go.'

Mary Ann stared into the darkness, waiting breathlessly for the silence to end. And when Mr. Lord's voice broke it, it was so low and quiet that she could scarcely make out his words.

'Very well; you go, Mr. Ratcliffe.'

Now came Ratcliffe's voice in a spate of words, forcing their way up through the blocked-in chimney and into Mary Ann's ear, so loud and so rapid that she could distinguish none of them until their speed lessened. And then they came slower than was ordinary and filled with such scorn that she was thrown on to the defensive.

'Your smallholding! You fancy yourself as a gentleman farmer. Why, the piggeries in my last job were bigger than this.'

'Doubtless. Then can you leave the smallholding as soon as possible?'

The tone should have shrivelled Mr. Ratcliffe dead.

'I am due for three months' notice.'

'Your money will be paid to you. I want you off my farm at the earliest possible moment.'

A door banged, and no more sound came up through the chimney. Mary Ann wriggled back along the beam and sat down. Mr. Ratcliffe had got the sack, not her da. The loft became filled with light. It streaked between the bales; it was not due to the sun coming out, but to the turn of events. Mr. Lord was going to keep her da on; Mr. Ratcliffe was going; they'd get a new manager, and he'd be nice ... he must be nice.

Mr. Ratcliffe had classed the farm as a smallholding. She wasn't exactly sure what this was, but it was something only as big as his last pigsties. She got to her feet. The sickness had left her chest and in its place was a bubbling joy. She'd dash down and tell her da, and then her ma. Oh yes, she must fly and tell her ma. And their Michael ... Michael wouldn't know till the night. And Lena Ratcliffe would soon be gone and she wouldn't have to put up with her swanking any more.

Almost bursting with excitement, she reached the top of the ladder, only to find her escape cut off for the time being, for there was Mr. Lord talking to Len, and by the sound of Mr. Lord's voice Len was getting it. .... But she must get down somehow and let her da know.

A suggestion of a means of escape rising in her mind turned her about, and she looked towards a square of floorboard with a ring in the middle. That was where they dropped the things through. Her da would be just under there, for she could hear him now calling to Jones to start her up. That would be the machine they were cleaning. She'd have to shout to him before they got that going or he'd never hear her.

Scampering to the trapdoor she pulled at the ring. But her effort made no impression. And then she laughed to herself as she looked down at her feet. How could she open it, she was standing on it? But much to her consternation she found that when she stood outside the trapdoor she couldn't reach the ring.

In a flurry now, she knelt down at the opposite side to

where it was hinged and, into the gap made by the countless hands that had grabbed its edge, thrust her own hands and pulled. And behold, the door came upwards towards her. But only for a short way, for she hadn't the strength to give it the final lift that would throw it back. This she decided didn't really matter, for she knew what she would do. She'd squeeze her head and shoulders in and call to her da . . . 'Sst! sst!' Like that.

Lying flat, she forced her head into the aperture, and then her shoulders, and from this unusual angle she looked down into the barn. The new aspect of the familiar place stilled her cry – things looked funny. She was looking on to the side of the binder. It was all sharp knives – shiny, sharp knives – and through them she could see her da at the other side of the machine bending down and rubbing something. The open door of the barn looked as if it was stuck to the ceiling; everything was topsyturvy.

She said, 'Sst!' And when Mike looked about him, not knowing from where the voice was coming, she gurgled inside and let him return to his job before putting her tongue to her teeth again. But the instant she did this, Mike's voice called, 'Let her go', and her 'Sst!' was drowned by the terrific noise and whirl of the blades beneath her. She became frozen with terror, and powerless to pull herself into the loft again.

Suddenly she screamed, a long piercing scream that cut into the din below and brought Mike's eyes upwards and paralysed his senses for a moment. From where he stood her threshing arms seemed to be waving directly over the machine. With a gabbled cry that re-echoed around the barn he sprang forward. His cry was to Jones and said 'Shut her off!' His right hand, emphasizing his demand, was thrust towards Jones, and his left, in a blind instinctive movement to save, towards the machine.

Mary Ann's eyes, already blinded by her fear, were now only able to take in part of what was happening, but piercing through her terror was the knowledge that her da was hurt. And when the machinery stopped and she heard his deep tearing groans and saw him staggering back against the barn wall clutching something red and running to his chest, her own screams filled her head and her body. Her world became swamped with nothing but her screaming. Even when she felt her legs gripped and she was being lifted into someone's arms, she still saw the barn and heard the groans. And to her screaming she added her struggles. She fought frantically to free herself, tearing like a wild animal for release.

'Me da! Me da! Me da! Me da!' It was as if her lungs drew fresh strength with each scream. . . . 'Me da! Me da! Me da! Me da!'

There were other arms about her, and she was dimly conscious of Mr. Lord's voice commanding her to cease her screaming. But she would not listen to it; she continued to fight and struggle and scream, always aiming to turn towards the barn.

Later, she knew she was in the kitchen and lying between the warmth of her mother's breasts and being rocked and rocked, always rocked. When the screams came the rocking would start. And then quite suddenly they both stopped, the rocking and the screams.

CHAPTER NINE

ABSOLUTION

MR. LORD stood in the kitchen with his back to the fire and looked from one to the other of the cheap pieces of furniture with which he had become very familiar during the past week. For instance, he knew that there were only eight blue roses bordering the saucers arrayed on the delf-rack, whereas there were nine on each of the tea plates. He knew that although there was a felt pad under the table cloth covering the little dining table, the top was badly marked. He knew also that one of the chairs had a short leg, which irritated him whenever it was his misfortune to sit on it. The furniture displeased him, and was saved from his utter condemnation only because of its scrupulous cleanliness.

He raised his eyes to the ceiling and moved uneasily. They were a long while up there. As he lowered his gaze again it touched on a farm calendar which said Monday, 14th March: Gregsons for all Farm Machinery. . . . Machinery. He turned abruptly towards the fire. It was almost a week to the very minute since all this trouble had started. Never would he want another week like it. And what was to be the outcome of it? A man with only one hand and a child half crazy? Of the two it was the child for whom he was more concerned. Something would be done for Shaughnessy. What he did not as yet know, farm work being now out of the question. But what could be done for the child, the child who had come, despite the persistent denials to himself, to be of an almost overpowering interest in his life? For nearly five days she had been kept asleep, and now, although she was awake and quite conscious, she was as lifeless as a rag doll.

The kitchen door opened and Lizzie entered, followed by the doctor.

After waiting a moment, Mr. Lord said, 'Well?'

The doctor drew on his gloves before replying. 'If it's possible, I advise that the father be brought home. I cannot see an improvement in her until he is.'

'But it's only a week, will they allow him out so soon?' he asked.

'I can find out. He can attend the out-patients' ward. If he can come out perhaps you'll be good enough to pick him up.'

The doctor's manner was brusque, and under other circumstances Mr. Lord's hackles would have risen and his own brusqueness would have overshadowed the doctor's. But on this occasion he said nothing, only followed him outside.

Lizzie stood at the window and watched them crossing the yard. In their ways they were both like gods. Mr. Lord had the power of their material future in his hands, and on the doctor Mary Ann's mental state seemed to depend. He was right, she knew, to bring Mike back, for only through him could Mary Ann become alive again. But the Mike she had seen yesterday was not the man who could inspire life in a child, or in anyone else. Her husband had always been a virile man. He had, she knew, been proud of his physique, of his tall, thick body, and of his strength, which drink had not yet impaired. Many a time he had picked her up bodily and held her aloft, glorying in his power to do so. But now, like a Samson without his hair, the loss of his hand had seemingly cut the virility out of him – he had appeared to her like a child.

'What am I do to, Liz? What job can I do with one hand, other than night watchman? That would kill me, Liz. They won't give me compen, it was me own fault.' He had not said it was Mary Ann's fault, and she knew he would not say so. And he must not. All blame must be taken from the child. Mary Ann must never be allowed to take to herself the blame for the loss of his hand. It was this guilt, she knew, that was hovering in the drugged layers of the child's mind, and only Mike, the old hearty Mike, could push it so far down that it would never rise again.

The door opened and Michael came in. He appeared to have grown older and taller during the past few days. He stood looking at her and stretching his school cap between his hands.

'What does he say?' he asked.

'That your da must come home,' she said.

'Ma.'

'Yes.'

'I'm going to leave school when I'm fifteen.'

'All right,' said Lizzie dully, 'there's plenty of time to talk about that.'

'But I am.' His tone was emphatic, yet held a tremor. And she looked at him and was touched at the trouble she saw in his face.

'And for as long as we're here I'm going to get paid for what I do on the farm, nights and weekends.'

'Who says so?'

'Mr. Lord. . . . Ma.'

'Yes?'

She saw that he was unable to speak, and he turned from her and hid his face in his arms against the wall.

Gently she pulled him round to her and pressed his head against her shoulder. She knew he was torturing himself, taking the primary blame because he had sent Mary Ann to listen. He sniffed hard and pulled away from her.

'She'll be all right,' she said, 'and your da'll get well. . . .

And Michael . . . when he comes home, and he may be home today, be . . . be nice to him, will you?'

He did not answer, but sat down on the fender and looked into the fire. . . .

Mike came home at three o'clock, and Mr. Lord, using an unused but natural tact, found something to busy himself with in the car. And so Mike came in alone. Like that of a man who had undergone a severe illness, his skin was shades lighter than was natural, and his eyes, sunk in his head, looked big and dark . . . and dead. Smiling her greeting, Lizzie put her arms about him, taking care of the arm strapped to his chest. And when only the pressure of his one hand touched her, leaving her body somehow cold, all her resolutions to put on a brave face vanished.

'Come on, come on,' he muttered gruffly. 'Stop your bubbling, I'm not dead yet.'

It sounded so much like the old Mike that she raised her eyes to his face, but it was still the face she had come to know during the past week. She drew away from him, and, trying to adopt a light tone, she said, 'Come and have a cup of tea.'

He sat down like a stranger by the side of his own table, and he had drunk half the tea before Mr. Lord put in an appearance.

'Can I offer you a cup of tea, sir?' asked Lizzie.

'Thank you, I'd like one very much.'

He, too, sat down by the table, and the room became as quiet as though there was no one in it. . . .

Upstairs Mary Ann lay looking at the elephants on the wall. They were not running after the giraffe and butting him with their trunks as they usually did when she concentrated her gaze upon them; they were standing stock still as paper elephants should do. She turned her head slowly and looked across the room. It seemed very big now that the curtain had been drawn back. The sun was shining through the little window and making a square of colour on the mat. But it was just the sun shining into a poorly furnished bedroom. It was no longer the most wonderful room in the world set in the best cottage in the world. It was drab and colourless, and she was aware of it. And it was this awareness that was partly the cause of the pain that was in her head and in her chest, for her life had been stripped of wonder.

When she had woken from the funny sleep the screaming was still in her head. If she kept her eyes open it wasn't so loud; but it was difficult to keep her eyes open. And then gradually it had died away, and in the strange quiet that followed she knew what she had screamed about. Since she had been awake no one had mentioned her da to her, her ma, or Mr. Lord, or the doctor, or their Michael. She knew why; because they were frightened to. She was waiting for someone to say, 'Your da's gone away on a long journey and you'll see him again some day.' That's what they said to Mary Fitzgerald when her da died. Mary had told them all in the school yard. But Mary Fitzgerald hadn't caused her da . . . to go away, whereas she had. Because she had almost fallen through the roof her da had . . . gone away, and she wouldn't see him again ever, not till she died. But now no suggestion came to her as to how she could bring about her demise; even this faculty was dormant. She looked at the foot of the bed where, on a bamboo table, stood her little altar. Her eyes rested on the figures of Our Lady and the Infant. They brought no solace. If any emotion touched her it was resentment that they had let her do this thing, that their guidance and protection were fallible.

When her eyes were brought to the doorway by the dark bulk filling it, she looked at Mike for a moment without recognition. Then the scream, entering her head again, brought her hands to her mouth. But it did not escape, for Mike's voice saying, 'Hallo, there', stilled it.

The 'Hallo, there' was so ordinary – it was his usual greeting, and he was saying it. He was walking towards her. He sat on her bed and said it again. . . . 'Hallo, there.'

Her eyes moved from his face to the arm strapped across his chest, then up to his face again.

'Well, aren't you going to give me a kiss?'

She made no move, and Mike said, 'Here am I, come rushing out of hospital to see you, and all you do is sit there and stare. Aren't you pleased to see me?'

Slowly she pulled herself up. But still she did not speak. Then her hand moved to his arm and touched it, just below the elbow. She looked at him again, and he smiled; then her arms were about his neck, pulling him towards her, and whatever pain he suffered by her contact with the raw stump of his wrist he gave no sign of it.

'Da. Oh, Da!'

'Now, what's all the fuss about?' He stroked her hair and talked to her as she lay quivering but dry-eyed against his breast. 'Here you are in bed with a cold when you should have been downstairs helping your ma to get the tea ready for me coming home. . . . And you never came to the hospital to see me, and there was me waiting every day. And all I could hear was, "She's in bed with a cold." So I said to meself, "Well, if she can't come to me I'm going to her . . . a bit cut on the hand's not goin' to keep me in bed." '

It all sounded very brave and airy. It was make-believe such as Mary Ann herself would have used. Yet he felt better for having said it. It was the first time he had actually referred to his hand. He had forbidden his mind to touch on it, and it had obeyed him except during his sleep, when he would dream that his hand was being sliced off his body . . . but slowly; and he would awake, thinking, My God! what a dream, only to realize that the dream was reality. And there would follow a period of retrospection, when he would go over his life and ask why everything he touched had the mark of failure on it. Was it the heritage from the parents he had never known? Or was it due to his ingrained sense of inferiority born of his life in a Cottage Home? Whatever the cause, his efforts seemed doomed. He had come to the farm with the firm intention of making a go of it, and nobody but himself knew what it had cost him those first few months to go without his drink. And then Quinton had to crop up again. Quinton, in himself, might be a decent enough fellow, but his very name had the power to show up his own shortcomings; and the knowledge that Quinton had loved Liz, and that had she married him her life would have been smooth and free from the perpetual worry she now knew, had been enough to raise the tearing demon of his jealousy.

But his troubles could have been halved, he knew, had he been able to conquer his weakness for the bottle.

Lying in hospital the future had seemed so dark that he could see not even the smallest ray of light. What lay before him but public assistance, the very thought of which brought his teeth grating over each other. There would be no compensation for the accident, it had been his own fault. He would not say Mary Ann's. . . . He could not think blame on the child who would sell her soul for him, but he knew that if her head had not come through the trap-door he would have his hand now. And they all knew it. Especially the old man. The old fellow might be fond of Mary Ann, but he would not fork out a couple of thousand for which she was the cause. And he wouldn't keep him on the farm. What good would he be on the farm, anyway?

The thoughts had revolved on each other, creating a fear. And there had been only one person to whom he could voice it . . . Liz. And she had pooh-poohed it.

'That's nothing,' she had said, 'we'll manage somehow. It's the bairn we must think of. She knows she's to blame, and it's doing something to her.'

He looked down now on the small white profile. It had done something. There was no spark of the old Mary Ann here. She was not even crying as she was wont to do with joy or sorrow. Talk about your hand, the doctor had said. Make light of it to her. It will help to balance her, and indirectly, yourself, too.

It was all right for them to ladle out advice. Nobody should give advice unless he had been in the same boat. . . . He wetted his lips, cleared his throat, and made an effort:

'You've got a stupid bloke for a da, haven't you?'

Her head pressed closer to him.

'I was never much good at anything, was I? Wouldn't listen to anybody, always the big fellow.' He felt sick at himself for talking this stuff, but as her head moved and her face was lost in his waistcoat he went on, 'Jonesy warned me. "You'll get your hand off one of these days," he said, "cleaning while the machine's on." . . . Well' – he stopped and the sigh he gave was not altogether feigned – 'Jonesy was right. I wouldn't listen. Third time's catchy time, Jonesy said, and it was. It served me right, I suppose. The only thing I'm sorry for is' – again he paused – 'that you had to be up in the loft and see it.'

Her head came up from his chest, and she looked at him, taking in this new aspect of the situation; and her spirit, gazing from her eyes, beseeched him to still her conscience for ever. Of its own accord, it demanded that he do for her what she was continually doing for him. It demanded now that he lie with the sincerity of sacrifice and redeem something of himself in absolving this child from all blame.

Words came to him, flowing with the smoothness of heavenly-endowed truth. He listened to himself uttering them, not knowing from where they sprang. And as he talked he saw the shadow of his Mary Ann return. It came back into her eyes; the sand-dryness became moist, and slowly she began to cry.

The new picture of her da, incompetent with machinery, stubbornly refusing all advice, even spurning the guiding hand of Mr. Ratcliffe, and admitting that any farm flair he had lay entirely with animals, brought her protective instinct surging up, and as it came it pressed down the numbing guilt into the secret chambers of her mind.

'Oh Da!' Her hand moving along his arm to where the neatly crossed bandages began. And again she said, 'Oh Da.'

'Look,' he said, 'I want cheering up. What you goin' to do about it? Are you coming downstairs with me?'

She hesitated.

'Come on, stand up.'

Obediently she stood up, rocking on her feet. Slipping his good arm about her he gathered her to him, and carried her down the stairs.

CHAPTER TEN

THE DEAL

ALTHOUGH Mary Ann's conscience was at rest once more, her mind was still troubled, for the anxiety that was eating into both Mike and Lizzie could not fail to make itself felt by her. Her da's pay packet had been brought to the cottage as if he was working, and Mr. Lord himself had said, 'Don't worry.' But she could feel that this statement instead of soothing her da's anxiety had only irritated him.

Mike did not want to be pensioned off out of charity. He wanted to work. At what? He didn't as yet know. He attended the out-patients' department; he read the 'wanted' columns; he gazed for hours out of the window in the direction of the farm; and he chafed at his lot. Finally and boldly, he approached Mr. Lord, saying, 'I'm not ungrateful, sir, but I can't go on like this.'

'Like what?' Mr. Lord had asked. 'You have been out of hospital for only ten days and I understand you have to attend for some time yet.'

'That's all very well,' said Mike, 'but what's to follow?'

Mr. Lord had given no direct answer to this question; all he said was to go home and rest and wait.

What was to follow Mr. Lord did not himself know. He had been racking his brains as to what course he should take. If he gave him a small lump sum and let him go, the child would go. Yet how to give him a job? He would, of course, eventually get a hook for his hand, but even then would he be able to do a day's work with the other men? It was very doubtful. To use a hook skilfully needed long practice, and his knowledge of men was too wide to think that their present sympathy for Shaughnessy would stand the test of years. Nor would a man like Shaughnessy tolerate being carried. No, he could not see Shaughnessy back on the farm. His labour troubles were bad enough without adding to them.

For the first time Mr. Lord regretted his farm venture; he regretted the expensive house he was building; he regretted very much paying Ratcliffe three months' money in lieu of notice and leaving the farm without a directive; and above all he regretted the incident that had caused a place in his heart to open when Mary Ann had boldly claimed him as her granda. Material things could be rejected or replaced, but when carefully guarded feelings were exposed to the light of a child's charm a man became vulnerable.

In mid-week Mary Ann suddenly expressed a desire to return to school, and Lizzie, without protest, let her go, for she felt that the atmosphere of the house was unhealthy for her. Daily, she witnessed Mike's attempt at cheerfulness when in Mary Ann's presence, and it hurt her. And she knew it hurt the child. For with Mike, Mary Ann was like a watchful mother – no shade of his feelings escaped her. She knew he was worried, so therefore she was worried.

It was Father Owen's unexpected visit that precipitated Mary Ann's return to school. As she sat listening to his cheerful talk in the kitchen she had wanted to pour out her troubles to him; but only in church or Confession could she do this. So she went back to school.

The reception she received from her class would, at any other time, have filled her with unholy pride. She would have grabbed at the opportunity to let her imagination have full rein, for had she not been hanging head first from a hole in the ceiling, with below a whirling machine and ten thousand blades ready to cut her up? And hadn't her da rushed in and saved her? The children themselves made it sound something like this, anyway; and in this instance she did not deny them the use of their imaginations. But she added nothing of her own. Her only comment, when in the playground one sympathizer said, 'Your poor da's got only one hand now,' was to add, 'That's nothing, he's still a grand man for all that.'

Let it be noted here that Sarah Flannagan did not attack this docile Mary Ann. After one scrutinizing look at her, she had walked off. This white, sapped-looking being was not a worthy recipient of her powers of invective.

There was no Confession on a Wednesday night, and Mary Ann knew that unless she bumped into Father Owen in the church there was no way of seeing him other than to go boldly to his front door and ask for him. But she didn't feel equal to making that effort now, for Miss Honeysett was a tartar. There was, however, always the Holy Family to fall back on.

So after school she went to them, not hitching or skipping, just walking. And when she knelt before them she found it was difficult to talk to them. Like everything and everyone else They had changed; They all had that 'gone away' look that her da had. She tried to commence in her usual way, but it was no good. She said a 'Hail Mary' and 'Our Father' and a 'Glory Be To God', but still her troubles would not flow. It was as if they were tightly locked within her and she had lost the key for their release. So she blessed herself, rose from her knees, and turned away, only to turn as quickly to them again, when her old self flashed through for a second as she implored 'Do something, will you?' But Their look of hurt surprise seemed to reproach her for her imperious demand and lack of faith, and her head drooped and she muttered, 'I am sorry', and to placate them, she added, 'Blessed be the Holy and Undivided Trinity now and for ever. Amen.'

Almost immediately upon this the vestry door creaked, and Father Owen, with a handkerchief to his nose, walked towards the altar. He stopped and sneezed twice, reached the bottom of the steps, genuflected, went up to the altar, lifted the heavy cross and descended the steps again. And there, through his streaming eyes he saw Mary Ann standing immediately in front of the altar rails, and having no regard for the millions of germs that he was letting loose on the world, and on Mary Ann in particular, he flapped his handkerchief at her and beckoned her towards the vestry. He sneezed as he put the cross down, and turning to her said, 'Oh, I'm in a right bad fix, aren't I; but it sounds much worse than it is. You're back at school then, Mary Ann?'

'Yes, Father.'

'That's good. Far better at school. And how's everything . . . all right?'

'Yes, Father . . . No, Father . . . No, it's not all right.'

'Oh dear! oh dear! Come and sit down. Have you had your tea? Of course you haven't, you haven't been home yet. Well, I've a bit of chocolate here.' He rummaged in his pockets, then exclaimed with astonishment, 'I've eaten it. I remember now, I've eaten it.'

'It's all right, Father,' she assured him unsmilingly, 'I've got some bullets in me bag.' She indicated her school bag hanging at her side.

He said, 'You're a clever girl to be able to save your bullets; meself, I'm a greedy hog and eat them as they come. How's your da?'

They were still standing looking at each other, but now Mary Ann's eyes dropped. 'His . . . his arm's getting better,' she said.

'That's good. He'll be as right as rain in no time and back to work.'

'What work, Father?' Her eyes were on his again.

Father Owen, peering at her over the top of his glasses, thought: That was a stupid thing to say. She's right, what work? A sneeze gave him a little breathing space and he dabbed at his nose as he asked, 'Has he said anything . . . what he wants to do or anything?'

'No, Father; but he keeps looking towards the farm.'

'Then he'll go back to the farm.'

'He says he won't . . . he can't.'

'Mr. Lord'll give him a light job, never fear.'

'Me da says there are no light jobs on a farm.'

'That's true . . . well, what I mean is, it's heavy work, farming.'

'Yes, Father.'

'Aye. Mm. Well . . .' Father Owen pushed his fingers through his thin hair. He was feeling in no mood to listen to troubles or to dole out advice. All he desired was to get his head down on a pillow; or one of his heads, for there seemed to be a dozen of them at the moment all spinning in different directions. But the child's face would haunt him if he left her in the air like this . . . bad stress to the man! He was always doing something to make her carry a weight much too heavy for her; yet, poor fellow, it wasn't his fault this time. He was to be pitied. He took a fit of coughing and when it was over he said, 'Oh this head of mine!'

'Does it ache, Father?'

'It does, it does. But as I was saying' – which he hadn't been saying – 'your da's a fine man and he'll get a job. Anyway, I think he'll be glad to leave the farm for he didn't take to the manager, did he?'

'No, Father.' Mary Ann's pleasure at the unsolicited compliment paid to her da was shining from her eyes. 'But Mr. Ratcliffe's gone, Father,' she said, 'and Lena an' all.'

'Gone?'

'Yes; he got the sack. He had a row with Mr. Lord.'

Father Owen was genuinely surprised at this news. He had been speaking to Peter Lord only yesterday and never a word had he said about losing his manager. Oh, the conceit of the old boy! He wouldn't let on he was having labour troubles on so small a place. He must be finding the farm as difficult to run as his yard. . . . A thought suddenly entering the priest's head made it wag and sent his eyes flickering over the vestry, and when finally they came to rest on Mary Ann they were screwed up into small points of light. 'Has your da got a good hand, Mary Ann?' To this faux pas he added, 'I mean, can he write nicely?'

'Oh yes, Father. He does me homework for me . . . me sums and things, and he writes lovely.' She paused – she had given herself away with a vengeance. But her uneasiness on this point was negligible. – Father Owen wouldn't split to Miss Thompson. She swallowed and added, 'He does write lovely.'

'Does he now? That's good. Well, do you know what I'm thinking?'

'No, Father.'

'I'm thinking he should go after a job where there's writing to do, but on a farm you know, buying and selling . . . a manager. That's what he should go after. Or something like that – perhaps an assistant to start with – for he's got a good eye for cattle, and but for the few years he spent in the yards he's been on farms all his life. Now that's what I advise. Of course, it would have to be a little farm.'

'But Father . . .' All her features were stretching away from one another in amazement at this suggestion.

'Now be quiet. I'm sure it would be the very thing. You see, Mary Ann . . . Come here.' He pulled her down on to the polished form that usually seated the scrambling altar boys when changing their shoes, and taking her hand, went on, 'Have you ever noticed it, Mary Ann, the way God works? If He wants to give you something He waits until you lose something. You see, everything in some way has got to be paid for. Do you know that, Mary Ann?'

'No, Father.'

'Well, it has. It's ten to one your da would never have thought of using his head to earn his living if he hadn't lost his hand. Now do you see?'

Mary Ann's eyes, although wide, were not seeing.

'It's like this,' said Father Owen. 'Leaving things as they were, your da would have remained a farmhand all his life, and content to do so; but then there was the accident, although mind' – the priest wagged a warning finger at her – 'God doesn't make accidents happen, you must remember that, Mary Ann. It's our foolishness and neglect that causes them. But when they do happen, in He steps and points out a way to bring happiness and contentment to the sufferer. Oh, I've seen it again and again. But of course it's no use His pointing out the way if we don't take advantage of it, is it?' He poked his head forward, and Mary Ann, beginning to see a dim light in the distance, said, 'No, Father.'

'It's up to us, Mary Ann, it's always up to us.' Here Father Owen took another bout of sneezing.

Mary Ann counted eight atishoos with concern; he sounded as if he was going to blow his head off. He was bad, poor soul, very bad.

After his streaming eyes had been dried, Father Owen began again, but a little heavily. 'As I was saying, farmers these days go to colleges and things, and that to my mind is a fanciful idea if ever there was one. Cows have given milk and lambs been born for many years now without the help of a college. And anyway your da could, if he gave his mind to it, pick up from books any added knowledge he wants, so why don't you ask him to have a shot at it, eh? Tell him not to aim at too big a farm, mind.' He turned his head a little to one side and glanced down at her. 'But one a bit bigger than Mr. Lord's . . . that's very small.' His nose wrinkled at the smallness of Mr. Lord's farm.

Mary Ann could not find it in her heart to be annoyed with this beloved friend who was also . . . bad, but her tone conveyed slight censure as she said, 'It's a nice farm, and not really little, not like a . . . smallholding. And it's bigger than a piggery, isn't it?'

Father Owen could not, of course, follow these comparisons, but he said, 'No, no, of course not,' to the first part, and 'Yes, yes,' to the second; then went on, a trifle wearily, 'There it is, that's what I advise your da to do. You needn't tell him I said so. Just put it in your own way and you'll see it will work out all right. Now, Mary Ann, my head's bursting and I'm going to me bed this very minute. . . . Do you feel any easier about things?'

'Yes, Father. I do, Father.'

And it was true. She did feel easier. There was a surging of the old excited feeling in her stomach. What she wanted now was to get to some place quiet, like bed, and think. So she said, 'Good night, Father. And I'll say a "Hail Mary" to Our Lady to look after your cold for you.'

The priest was laughing now as he cried, 'I don't want her to look after me cold, you stipulate that I want to get rid of it. Get on with you, now, home to your tea, and don't worry. Leave everything to God. Good night.'

'Good night, Father.'

He watched her for a moment from the vestry door, and as he turned away he put his hand to his head. What had he done this time? To put an idea into the head of that child was like supplying her with a bomb. Ah well, it was done. He only hoped that when she held the explosive under Mr. Lord's nose and put the match to it he would descend to earth again whole, which was asking for a miracle.

Mary Ann was feeling considerably better, for her mind was working. It was tackling a problem. She lay staring into the darkness. The house was quiet, but it was an uneasy quiet. No sound came from Michael behind the curtain, and across the landing the unrest was even greater, making itself evident by its complete stillness. There was no dim whisper of murmuring voices, not even a creaking bedspring or a cough. . . . The morrer, her da was going to tackle Mr. Lord finally. He had said so. And this was enough to cause her concern, for she knew that, left to themselves, the interview would not be successful – her da wouldn't knuckle under even in pretence to Mr. Lord. Without somebody, as she put it to herself, doing something, they would get on at each other.

She was also fully aware that the relationship between herself and Mr. Lord had shown little improvement; not even when she was bad had they got on to the old footing. He had been nice to her and sent her flowers and things, but he wasn't the same as when she had first come to the farm. No; he had wanted her to do something and she hadn't done it, and that had made him get his . . . back up. Also she was aware that she could not approach him using her old tactics; they would not carry weight with him now. Some new way, she felt, must be found if she was to carry out the scheme thought up by the Holy Family and suggested by Father Owen.

With a matureness beyond her years and accepted without question, she now realized that any success she could hope for with Mr. Lord would best be brought about by a frontal attack. As she so plainly put it to herself in the darkness: Tell him straight what you'll do for him if he'll do something for you. That was to be the strong structure of the scheme – exchange. What the exchange would mean to her she did not dwell on. First things first. If her da was settled, then her world would be all right . . . somehow.

She left for school as usual the following morning, but alighted from the bus at Pratt's Lane. This daring act alone made her knees weak, for she was about to play truant, and although she would tell Miss Thompson she had felt bad again and couldn't come to school, there was still Confession to be faced.

The door of Mr. Lord's house was open, and outside on the gravel drive was a car. It was painted blue and had a big dent in the mudguard, besides which it had no top. She had seen this car before. Only last night when she was going down the lane home it had come up from the farm. Why it should cause her uneasiness she didn't know, but it did. Ben explained the reason. He was mounting the stairs when her 'Psst!' halted him. He actually came down again and asked her how she was. His face wore his habitual look of disapproval but his voice had a touch of kindness. 'And how's your Father?' he inquired.

'He's not bad,' she said. 'Mr. Ben' – this was the title she had bestowed on him since Christmas – 'Mr. Ben, is The Lord with somebody?'

Ben nodded. 'He is. He's interviewing a young fellow who's after the farm manager's job. And there's another one due any minute. I wouldn't trouble him this morning . . . he's very busy.'

'Oh!' The bottom dropped out of her world. Her bright shining scheme became like a much-used comic . . . dull. Even the abrupt opening of a door to a room she had never entered and the appearance of Mr. Lord himself did little to lighten it. But immediately the owner of the blue car appeared in the doorway the scheme took on a glow again, faint, but nevertheless a glow. The young man wore knee breeches, polished gaiters, a lovely tweed coat, and he carried a short stick. Anything so unlike Lord's farm could not be imagined. Mary Ann's innate sense of fitness told her that he looked ... too swanky. And soon, also, she sensed the Lord's reactions, for his leave-taking of the man was peremptory, while the owner of the blue car was all but condescending.

Mary Ann's presence at that time of the morning caused Mr. Lord some surprise. He came back from the hall door before the owner of the old and battered but still impressive Jaguar had gone on his way.

'Hallo, what are you after, eh?' His tone was kindly, as if she was still sick.

'I want to talk to you.'

There was an exchange of glances between the old servant and his master as they remembered that these were the very same words she had spoken early one morning in this hall some months ago. Mr. Lord peered down on her. This was not the cheeky imp who had demanded audience with him that morning. This was an older Mary Ann, if a frailer one. He felt a strange longing for the battling, intrepid fighter, the loyal liar; and his tone was kind as he voiced his refusal. 'I'm busy this morning, I've got someone coming.'

'It won't take a minute ... well, not long.' Sincerely she prayed that it wouldn't take long.

Mr. Lord cleared his throat. 'Why aren't you at school?'

'I told you, I wanted to talk to you.'

There was only one thing that she would want to talk about, and he was in no mood to hear talk of Shaughnessy this morning. 'Later perhaps,' he muttered, and was visibly startled at the keenness of her perception when she said, 'It isn't only about me da.'

'No, then?' he asked. 'What is it?'

'Well ...' She hesitated. Ben was still standing there, and as her eyes involuntarily slid to him, he grunted and departed. Mr. Lord, glancing at his watch, said, 'Only a few minutes, mind.'

She trotted after him into the room he used as an office, and the lumber of books and papers that met her eye took her interest for a moment from the vital matter in hand. She stood looking round as Mr. Lord seated himself at his desk, and when he said, 'Well, what is this you have to tell me?' she turned to him and said, 'You want cleaning up.'

'What?'

She waved her hand round the room. 'It's mucky. Me ma would soon do it for you, she's a . . .'

'Yes, yes. Leave the room alone. What is this you want to say to me?'

She walked to his desk, and, standing at the side, lifted up a sheet of paper from the top of a pile of letters.

'Put that down!' His hand snatched the letter from her. 'Now, what is it you want?'

He was in a bad temper. If he got in a stew just because she touched his papers what would he do when she asked him about the farm job?

'Well?'

She looked up into the pale-blue eyes. They were the colour of the glass vase on the cottage mantelpiece, the one you couldn't see through. 'Do you still want me to go to that school?'

Mr. Lord made no immediate answer, but the swivel chair moved slowly round and brought him to face her.

'I'll go if you want me.'

There was not the slightest change in his expression. 'Since when have you wanted to go?'

'Since last night, in bed.'

'Why?'

' 'Cos I want to go . . . if . . .'

'Yes?'

'Well, if I do something for you, will . . .?'

'Will I do something for you?' he ended tersely.

'Yes.'

Mr. Lord drew in his breath and his head moved slightly. 'You don't think I'd be doing something for you by sending you to this school?'

'No – I mean – not what I want.'

'Then you don't really want to go to this school?'

'Yes . . . yes, I do.'

'Why are you willing to go?'

'Because you want me to.'

He leant a little towards her. 'You would go to please me?'

135

'Yes . . . if—'

He sighed again. 'If I did something for you?'

She could not find words to placate his tone, so she remained silent.

'What is it you want?' His voice was dull.

She stared at him. It had sounded quite an easy thing when in bed to say 'I'll go to this school on condition that you make me da manager,' but now the enormity of the request assumed its rightful proportions and she knew that the bargain was quite unequal; in fact, she didn't think she could bring herself to ask it.

'Well – come on.'

Her tongue was sticking to the roof of her mouth, and there it would have remained for some time no doubt had not the jangling sound of the front-door bell released it. That ring she knew was the . . . other fellow, so, gulping, she began, 'Me da must have a job. He wouldn't be happy anywhere else but on a farm, for he's grand with animals as you know. But now he can't use his hands . . . only the one. Mr. Ratcliffe didn't use his hands either; he never dirtied his hands. Me da said he was a book farmer and a hard day's work would have killed him. Me da's cleverer than Mr. Ratcliffe. He writes a good hand an' all, and he said last night he was going to . . . to . . .' She stopped. Where was it Father Owen said some farmers went? School? No, college.

Mr. Lord hadn't moved, but his expression had changed for the worse and Mary Ann's voice had a distinct tremble as she continued: 'To college or some such, where they learn to be managers.' Her voice was small now. 'There, that's it.'

Mr. Lord's colour had deepened and his brows were aiming to reach his pursed lips as he growled, 'What are you asking? That I should make your father manager of my farm?'

The 'my' carried a weight all its own, and Mary Ann's voice reached a croak as she said, 'He'd be a fine manager, and it's only a little farm – bigger than a smallholding though – but me da would work hard for you and I'd go to school for you and everything'd be all right.'

'Who put this idea into your head – your father?'

'No – he knows nothing about being a manager.' She

stopped; she was getting into deep waters, her father was supposed to be going to college.

'Father Owen?'

'Father Owen?' she repeated, as if for the first time in her life she had heard the name. 'Father Owen? No. I went to church and I prayed . . .'

'All right' – he held up his hand abruptly in protest – 'that's enough. Now' – he pushed back his thin shoulders – 'go along and forget all this business that you've hatched up. School and farm included. It's out of the question.'

'But—' she moved nearer to him.

'That's enough.' As they stared at each other a tap came on the door.

'What is it?' He looked towards Ben.

'Mr. Dukes, sir.'

'Show him in. . . . Now, off you go.' His manner of dismissal was neither of his usual ones. There was no flaring temper nor was his voice barking, it was quiet, but not kindly quiet. It left no vestige of hope that might guide her back to a point from where she could resume her attack; there was a dead finality about it.

As she went out, Mr. Dukes came in, and had she been possessed of hope it would have fled on the sight of the sturdy workaday-looking man. She could see this one on the farm, and coping.

The hallway was empty and she stood amidst its dim dustiness and gnawed at her thumbnail, and as she gnawed the tears came. Slow, painful tears; tears for her ma when she had to leave the cottage; tears for their Michael, unsettled once again and morose; but most of all there were tears for her da and the sadness piled up within him. She heard the creak of footsteps on the landing above and she moved back and stood in the dark corner by the panelling that flanked the broad stairs. Ben came downstairs and went into the kitchen, but she did not move towards the hall door. Whether by accident or design she was standing right opposite the office door and she could hear the voices in the room rising and falling. But from where she stood it was impossible to hear what they were saying, so she cautiously moved nearer, taking the precaution to hold her nose so that she wouldn't sniff. Her head bent to the keyhole, the voices came as clear as if she were in the room, yet what they were saying was like a foreign language to her, and not really connected with the job for a farm manager. And most distressing of all, the voices were friendly. First the man's, talking about pigs at twenty-eight shillings a score. She knew what a score was – it was twenty, so that meant you could get twenty pigs for twenty-eight shillings. And twenty hundredweights of protein, the man said.

They were talking like sums at school, and then Mr. Lord's voice. 'Seven shillings a week on wages,' he was saying, 'and it won't stop there.' 'Land Race. They were the ones,' the man said. Then, 'Wheat at twenty-two and eightpence, with a good fertilizer. . . . And a sprayer attachment.' Mr. Lord's voice, quiet now, saying it wasn't paying its way. Then no more from Mr. Lord, and the man going on and on. Potash, nitro-chalk, winter feed. Then the miracle. He kept on about the miracle. Mary Ann never knew that miracles were needed to get milk from cows, but apparently they were, and they were attached to a bucket milker.

The voices droned on, mostly the man's, but both were still friendly. They even laughed together. The sound of the laughter must have dulled her senses for she was unaware that the voices had ceased, and the next thing she knew was that the support of the door left her and she was on her knees with a pair of feet on either side of her. Her startled glance darted from one set of boots to the other. Then an exclamation from the man drowned by a roar from Mr. Lord shot her to her feet, and without raising an eye to either of them she was off and out of the door and down the drive. As she ran, panting, towards the gate, the bus passed, then stopped, and when she reached the road the bus conductor called, 'Come on, divvn't hang aboot.'

She got on, assisted by his hand on her collar, and not till she was seated did she realize that she was bound Jarrowwards. And she didn't want to go to Jarrow, someone might see her and ask her why she wasn't at school. But it was done now. She could, she decided after some thought, go to Mrs. McBride's till dinner time, and perhaps she would get a bite of dinner there as she would miss her school dinner. This settled, she left the bus, not at her usual stop, but near Burton Street, to where she slowly made her way.

It was unfortunate that outside Mackintosh's shop at the corner she should come across a number of under fives playing the game of mothers and fathers. It was a different version altogether from her own in that they had a live set of twins to give authenticity to the game. These were being forced, at the hands of a distracted four-year-old mother with a running nose, to sit on the cold pavement, but, as the twins were the ripe and obstinate age of two years and one had a large rent in her knickers which made contact with the pavement still less desirable, a howling match was in progress.

Mary Ann, with time on her hands and unable, even at this stage of mental unrest, to pass anyone who so obviously stood in need of advice, stopped to add the wisdom of her years to the slight knowledge of the new mother. And she was doing it quite effectively when her arm was caught in an extremely tight grip and she was swung about to face, of all people at this time of the morning, Sarah Flannagan.

'What you doing here?' Sarah glared at Mary Ann, and any feeling of sympathy that the general attitude had forced her to show towards Mary Ann was swept away by the sight of her enemy, apparently herself again, playing happily in the street in school hours, and, what was more, in their street!

'Mind your own business,' said Mary Ann quietly.

This polite reply, it must be admitted, was mainly due to surprise, for of all the people she would wish to avoid this morning, Sarah Flannagan came first.

'Pretending you're bad,' said Sarah, 'and playing in the street.'

'I'm not.'

'You are.'

'Well, what you doing?' said Mary Ann, still quietly. 'If you weren't out playing you wouldn't see me.'

'I'm not out playing, so there, clever cuts. I've been about me teeth, to have a wire on. See?'

Sarah let Mary Ann see. She bared her teeth and pushed her face down to Mary Ann's level, and Mary Ann, after gazing wide-eyed at the row of large uneven teeth banded by wire, turned away and gave a vivid and audible imitation of vomiting, whereupon Sarah advanced upon her, crying,

'You! get back to where you belong, the pigsties. Me ma says you won't be long there either, you're all going to get the push.'

'What!' Mary Ann rounded on her, her old self flashing into life now that her family once more were being attacked. Her body stretched, her chin jutted, and she cried, 'You! You and your ma! You know nothing. I wouldn't be found dead in the same back lane. You're jealous because of our fine house; and me da, fine and respected. . . .'

'Oh my good garden cabbage!' This was Sarah's equivalent, of 'God in Heaven!' or 'God Almighty!' exclamations which were strictly forbidden by Mrs. Flannagan. But Sarah put so much into the words that they took on the strength of blasphemy and enraged Mary Ann still further. She flew at Sarah, knocking the temporary mother of the twins on to her bottom in her rush, and standing so close to Sarah as almost to touch her, she barked up into her face, 'You'll get the shock of your life, you will, you'll see! Me da's going to be a gentleman – a real one – a manager, and run a farm, and carry a stick and wear shiny leggings. And I'm going to be a lady, I am, a real lady, and talk nice. So stick that up your neb and blow your nose!'

Mr. Lord need not have mourned the loss of the battling intrepid fighter; she apparently had been merely sleeping. Mary Ann suddenly felt better, much better. Joined now to her yelling was the yelling of the twins, the shouts of the pretending mother and the four other accessories to the family tree. The noise having gone beyond the usual limit, the shop door was pulled open and two women appeared, one being the mother of the twins, the other Mrs. McBride.

'In the name of God,' cried Fanny, 'is it another war? Hallo, Mary Ann,' she said in surprise, 'what you up to?'

'It's her,' Mary Ann's voice was drowned by the cries of the real mother and her offspring, but her finger, pointing to Sarah's now retreating figure, made everything clear to Fanny, who exclaimed, 'Aye, it would be.'

The mother of the twins being totally blind to her children's smell, dirt and general ugliness, was now embracing them and bestowing on them such adjectives as beautiful and lovely. And as she trailed them away on one side of the street, Mary Ann and Fanny walked down the other, and as they went, Mary Ann, docile now, told Fanny she was playing truant.

'And why?' asked Fanny, definitely puzzled.

'I can't tell you outside,' said Mary Ann.

Once inside Mrs. McBride's odourful kitchen, Mary Ann proceeded to tell why she was off school. The telling of it was a little mixed, but this much was clear to Fanny, the child had the nerve of the devil. She may have had a shock over Mike's business, but it had deprived her of nothing, least of all her nerve, that she could see.

'You asked him to make your da manager?' she said. 'Be God! you've got big ideas. No wonder he sent you packing. What made you think your da could do such a job; it takes Mike all the time to manage hissel'?'

'It doesn't. He could . . . he could do it fine; anything fine.' Now her head was jerking and Fanny, her great hand making conciliatory motions in the air, said, 'All right, all right. Don't shout. I'm not saying a word against your da. You know I wouldn't. I'm the best friend he's got, for that matter, but there's limits to all things. It was a miracle he got the job and you know it was, and now you're expecting not only a miracle but a visitation. Be God! child, don't you realize that old Lord's no fool, no yard owner is, and if he's taken a farm it's to make money. And although I know nothing of farms, even if me grannie did keep a pig and ten ducks in the back-yard until some delicate-nosed neighbour kicked up a stink, I know this much: the way they run farms these days takes a headpiece. You've only got to look at the milk bottles with their "pasteurized" and their "T.T.s" to know that behind the cow there's brains.'

'Me da's got brains.'

'He has, he has an' all, and I'd be the first to admit it, but there are brains and brains, and you need a special kind of brains on a farm. And what about this being a lady? Are you going to that school?'

'No, not now.'

'Well, it's just as well as I see it. I can't see you settling in a place like that. You're not cut out for it, hinny,' she patted Mary Ann's lowered head. 'You're too like God made you, and I wouldn't like to see you spoilt. No, hinny, stay as you are; don't let them put any artificial manure on you, an' all.'

'Mrs. McBride.'

'Aye?'

'What's me da going to do?'

Fanny looked down on to the still bowed head, and after a moment she said, 'I don't know, hinny. But do as I do, don't worry. Leave it to God, and He'll see you're all all right, as He has done me.' She looked round her room; it was full of the remnants of furniture battered and torn by children's hands and feet. No one could have been persuaded to take the lot as a gift, yet their possession and the memories they stored were, to Fanny, gifts from God; and in these gifts she was happy.

'Let's have a sup of tea,' she said. 'Eh? It'll get your old spunk up. Come on, wash up me cups and don't worry no more about your da. He's like the cats, he'll fall on his feet.'

'Why,' asked Miss Thompson, 'weren't you at school this morning?'

'I was sick.'

'You weren't sick.'

Mary Ann stared back at her teacher. Sarah had got her oar in.

'You'll get your mother to write me a note and bring it to me in the morning.'

'Yes, Miss Thompson.'

Mary Ann had expected much worse treatment than this, for Miss Thompson was a hard nut. The light sentence made her buoyant; and at play-time she boldly went up to Sarah and said, 'So, clever stick, you thought you'd get me wrong with Miss Thompson. Well, you didn't. She said it was all right. And she asked after me ma. You're so sharp you'll cut yersel' one of these days.'

Mary Ann had completely recovered.

Sarah's retort was stifled by the appearance of the teacher, but her look said, 'You wait', and Mary Ann, correctly interpreting the look, was not surprised when school was over to see a reception committee waiting for her outside the gate.

Accompanied by Cissie and Agnes, she was met by Sarah.

and four of her friends. They too had forgotten that only last week they had said, 'Poor Mary Ann's da.' Now Mary Ann Shaughnessy was once again a cheeky thing and a big liar, added to which she was getting swanky. They allowed the three of them to pass, then in a concerted chant they sang.

> 'Pig-sty Annie,
> Snout in trough,
> Tongue too long she'll bite it off.'

But this was not strong enough to turn Mary Ann about. What was more, she was remembering her mother's caution against fighting, a caution she had completely overlooked earlier in the day. So, with an exaggerated wobble of her small hips, she marched down the street flanked by her two aides. Not even when the chant became decidely vulgar, dealing liberally with the anatomy of a cow, and comparing the same with Mary Ann's face, did she turn.

This aloofness was much too much for Sarah, and drove her to resort to the lethal weapon of Mike. After running to get closer to the tormentor of her dreams and flesh, Sarah yelled to her own cronies, 'Do you know something? Me da's a grand man. He gets bottled up every Saturday night and dances in the street; and he's had the sack umteen times and he's going to get the push again.'

Before she finished Sarah had gained her objective; Mary Ann had turned. But, against all procedure, she did not retaliate with her tongue – the cruelty of Sarah's words stilled her own but aroused such a protective passion in her for the maimed hero of her world that had Sarah been as large as an elephant she would still have attacked her.

In the mêlée that followed, when she found herself pinned against the lamp-post with her feet alone free, she used them, and for every blow she received across the face and head she gave Sarah one lower down, until her legs too were caught and held by one of the enemy.

'Now we'll see,' cried Sarah, hopping on one leg and glaring into Mary Ann's flaming face. 'I've got you now, and I'll give you something you won't forget ... you and your da! the big, dirty, drunken lump. .... Manager indeed! There, take that! A gentleman with gaiters! And that and ...'

'Stop it at once!'

The children all turned their eyes towards the kerb from where the harsh command had come.

'Get away, you hooligans!'

As they saw the old man make to get out of the car, Sarah and her army got away, leaving a stunned Mary Ann and two equally stunned followers.

Mr. Lord, on the pavement now and waving his arm towards the car, cried, 'Get inside!' However much he may have been concerned for her it certainly did not show in his voice, or yet in his expression.

Mary Ann staggered into the car, but once on the seat she turned and looked at her dishevelled supporters, and in a small voice, she asked, 'Can they come an' all? Will you drop them?'

'No!'

With a feeling of having deserted her wounded comrades Mary Ann was driven away, and not until the car had left Jarrow did Mr. Lord speak, and then only in the nature of a growl.

'You are a hooligan,' he said.

Mary Ann did not attempt to defend herself. She was too concerned at the moment with the condition of her face, which seemed to be growing larger with every second. Her whole head pained and throbbed, and only strong control and the knowledge that Mr. Lord had no use for bubblyjocks stopped her from crying. But even the desire to cry was forgotten when Mr. Lord, pulling the car into the side of the road, stopped it, and turning to her said, 'I want to talk to you.'

She lifted her swelling eyes up to him. There was something wrong here, for that was what she always said.

'Are you listening?'

'Yes.'

'Do you know what you asked me to do this morning?'

'Yes.'

'Well, I'm going to do it.'

Her eyes like pop-alleys devoured his face; then, 'You are?' she whispered.

'Yes; but on my conditions.'

She did not ask what these conditions were but waited without a blink of an eyelid for him to go on.

His brows beetling, his whole expression forbidding, he continued, 'I'm going now to offer your father the post that you asked for him, but he's not to know that you suggested it, or that you offered to go away to school. Is that clear?'

Slowly she nodded.

'Is it quite clear?' he asked.

'Yes.'

'What have you to do?'

'I . . . I haven't to let on to me da that I got him the job.'

'Not ever,' he said.

'Not ever,' she repeated.

'And you haven't to mention going away to school. . . . But you are going away to school,' he added with emphasis. 'Don't forget that, mind.'

'No,' she said.

'But you are not to mention a word of it yet. In a few days time you can suddenly make up your mind that you want to go . . . you understand?'

'Yes.'

'Are you quite sure now?'

'Yes. I'll suddenly say, "I want to go to that school 'cos I want to learn French and things." And I'll say it's – it's because I want to be like or better'n Lena Ratcliffe and show Sarah Flannagan a thing or two. That would do, wouldn't it?'

'Yes, I suppose so; something like that.'

Mr. Lord mopped his brow and leaned back in his seat. All this business was very tiring; it had been a tiring day altogether. If anyone had told him first thing this morning that by this evening he would have come to the decision of offering Mike Shaughnessy the management of his farm he would, to say the very least, have termed that person mad. And here he was, not only proposing to offer Shaughnessy the job, but manoeuvring it so that he would be more likely to accept it, for he knew the man sufficiently by now to understand that were he to offer him the post because the child had asked it he would be just as likely to refuse it – he knew he had been given his present job solely for the child's sake, and in a man of his calibre, it had rankled. And now, should the stubborn, pig-headed red-head, through any pretext whatever, dare to turn down the offer he himself was

145

mad enough to make, the refusal would take the form of a personal defeat, and at his age he felt he would not be able to stand such a defeat.

He was becoming vulnerable; he needed people; this child, the warmth of her; he needed the occupation that her future moulding would take. But it wasn't only his need that had brought about the present crazy state of affairs, it was the events following on each other from early this morning; those two fellows who had come after the post, one a nincompoop, the other knew too damn much . . . he was a walking farm encyclopaedia who would be out to renew every item on the farm starting from the chickens and the byres to the combiner and the bull; and then later the incident on the farm . . . the men coming and asking him to keep Shaughnessy on and they'd level out the work. He had put a flea in their ears and asked who said he was going to dismiss Shaughnessy at all, and they had gone off looking a bit silly, and leaving him feeling equally silly, for he had placed himself in a difficult position. . . . What was he to do with the man? And all the time in the back of his mind he knew. And he knew it would give him a kick to do it. He also knew that Shaughnessy would be his for life after such an offer. It had always been his policy in the yards to give a difficult man a little responsibility. It had nearly always worked, and it would work again this time; that is, should Shaughnessy think the proposal came solely from him.

He looked down again on the gaping child.

'Do you understand that if your father thought I was giving him this job because you asked me, he would refuse it?'

After a moment she said, 'Yes . . . yes, I do.'

'And you'll never mention a word that you came to me about it?'

'No.'

'If you ever did it would make him unhappy and he would leave. Do you understand that?'

'Yes; I do understand.'

He looked into her wide eyes. Yes, she understood all right. There was little concerning the man and his reactions that she did not understand. Abruptly he turned to the wheel and started the car, and as they moved off Mary Ann moved up until she was close-pressed against his side. And there she remained until they reached the crossroads, where he said, 'Don't go in looking so pleased with yourself. You're a bad girl, don't forget. And I found you fighting.' He cast a sidelong glance at her, which was joined by a knowing gleam from her eye. She straightened up, shuffled on her bottom along the seat, and endeavoured by adopting a pained expression to subdue the bubbling excitement within her.

So they came to the back of the cottage and stopped opposite the kitchen window. . . .

'Here he comes,' said Mike over his shoulder to Lizzie, 'and he's got her with him. . . . I suppose this is it. He knows he can't keep dodging me for ever.' He turned from the window, characteristically bracing his shoulders back. Lizzie said quietly, 'Be careful, Mike.'

The request irritated him. He wanted to go for the old fellow, to say, 'Look here, tell me out what you mean to do, I want no more of this cat and mouse business.' But there were so many things to curb his tongue . . . a roof over their heads; the look on Liz's face; the lad going back into that quiet, secretive way of his. He did not bring Mary Ann into his worrying, for he knew whatever his fate she would remain the same, loving him, believing in him, his alone . . . no matter what the old boy tried to do.

It was towards her he looked when the door opened, and his eyes narrowed.

'What you been up to?' he demanded.

But before Mary Ann could answer, Mr. Lord, using his most truculent manner, said, 'Fighting . . . in the gutter . . . like a hooligan.'

Mike and Lizzie stared at Mary Ann, and she stared back at them before lowering her head.

'You should do something.' Mr. Lord was addressing Lizzie. 'Never seen anything like it . . . fighting tooth and claw . . . like animals.'

'I've warned you,' said Mike quietly, 'haven't I? Get up to bed.'

'Wait a minute,' said Lizzie; 'look at her face. How did it get like this?' she asked Mary Ann as she bent over her and took off her coat.

'Sarah Flannagan, with her hand,' muttered Mary Ann.

'I'm going to put a stop to this once and for all,' said Mike. 'Get up those stairs.'

He was making a demonstration for the old man's benefit, Lizzie knew.

'I'll have to wash her,' she said softly. 'Won't you sit down, sir?' She pulled a chair forward.

'No, no,' said Mr. Lord. 'I only want a word with your husband.'

Lizzie, casting a swift pleading glance at Mike, took Mary Ann's arm and propelled her into the scullery, and after closing the door behind them she asked, 'Where did all this happen?'

'Near the school, Dee Street end.'

Lizzie turned in the collar of Mary Ann's dress.

'It's got to stop, as your da says.'

Mary Ann could not assent to this, for the wet flannel was over her mouth.

'Did he say anything to you about your da?'

Mary Ann closed her eyes before the flannel reached them. She had to, so that she wouldn't see the anxiety in her mother's face, for with a word she could send it flying away. This event, she decided, was not going to be at all like the time her da got the job on the farm. Her da and ma had then acclaimed her, and she knew she was clever. But now, when she had to make on she knew nothing about it, all the fun would be gone. Well, nearly all; there still remained the fact that her da would be all right. . . .

Mary Ann, washed and dried, sat on the cracket, and Lizzie made a great to-do with the few dirty dishes, clattering them unnecessarily to deaden the sound of the voices from the kitchen, for the fear of what she would hear was heavy on her.

Mary Ann was not even bothering to listen, for quite suddenly she was feeling dizzy and a bit sick; but when the door was pulled open and her da stood there, she got to her feet. But Mike did not look at her, he looked at Lizzie, saying, 'Come in here a minute.'

Lizzie, drying her hands, went into the kitchen. She looked in open surprise at her husband's face, it was as if he had been reborn. The Mike she had left a few minutes earlier had been a dull, sullen man; here was a man with a light in his eye, such a light as she had not seen for many a long day. And his whole body had broadened again.

'Liz' – he spoke to her, but he looked towards Mr. Lord – 'Mr. Lord's going to give me the chance. . . .' He stopped and ran his hand over his mouth. Then he turned to her: 'He's going to let me run the farm as a trial for the next six months.'

Lizzie, bereft of words, her mouth slowly dropping into a gape, stared at Mr. Lord. Then she whispered, 'Oh sir! oh sir!'

'It isn't all it sounds,' the old man growled. 'It won't be easy, I promise you . . . in no way. There's the men. They might be willing to help you keep your job, but it'll be a different kettle of fish when you're giving them orders.'

'I'll do me best with them, and I'll work . . . I'll work, sir.'

Lizzie had never before heard that tone in Mike's voice.

'And I'll get books and things. I can do it if I like, I know I can. There's one thing I can promise you on my oath . . . you won't regret it. I'll work as never before. . . .'

'And keep sober?'

It was a direct shot, and Mike looked back into the old man's eyes for a long moment before saying, 'I'll do me best there an' all.'

Into the embarrassing silence that fell on the three of them came a revolting sound from the scullery. Mary Ann was in the process of being actually sick, and once more came into the picture.

CHAPTER ELEVEN

THE LAST WORD

THE whole school was stunned, weighed under the magnificence that was surrounding her. At least this was the impression that Mary Ann got, for had not her ma been to see the headmistress and told her she was going to leave and was going away to a posh school? And at dinner time her ma had met her outside the gates for everybody to see, and they had gone together to Mrs. McBride's. And her ma had taken a point end of brisket along, for Mrs. McBride liked to make broth with brisket. And she'd also given her a dozen oranges. And Mrs. McBride had pretended fine that it was all news to her what her ma was saying.

Eeh! it was a good job, Mary Ann considered, that she had remembered telling Mrs. McBride about going to Mr. Lord's and gone to her and told her not to let on. For the first thing Mrs. McBride would have done on meeting her ma or da would have been to joke about the nerve of her asking for the job.

After having looked funnily surprised for a long while Mrs. McBride had laughed and laughed, then hugged her. And she herself had felt a little appeased, for it was nice to have credit from someone.

The past four days had been odd, queer days. Their happiness had been outside her, not inside, not the kind of happiness she felt when her da thought her wonderful. Her da was happy, and her ma was happy, so was their Michael; they were going to move into the farmhouse. This last should have filled her with pure job; but it didn't, for she wouldn't be living in the farmhouse, only now and again. At night times she thought about it all, and to the time when she would be going away, away from her da for weeks on end, with only swanky people to speak to, very likely all the same as Lena Ratcliffe. She knew she would die when she got to that school; but she would have to go. Everything must be paid for, that's what Father Owen said.

Poor Father Owen; he was in bed with his cold. She'd braved Miss Honeysett and called at the house every day, but old Bumble Bee wouldn't let her inside the door. But as soon as school was over for the day she was going again, and if he was up she would ask to see him, for she had so much to tell him; not least her latest decision with regard to her future state, for she had decided quite finally that when she was finished with this school she was going on the pictures. This, she had concluded, would be quite easy for her to accomplish, for although with every breath she drew she acted, she had not consciously done so up to the last four days; and more so the day before yesterday when her da had spoken to her before she went to school, saying, 'Mind, I'm telling you, any more fighting in the street and you're for it.'

She had stood with her back to him looking towards the scullery door, and in that moment she had decided that the time was right to do as Mr. Lord had bidden her. So turning to him, she said, 'Da ... you know that school Mr. Lord wanted me to go to? Well, I want to go.' She remembered the look that came over his face, but she could not even now say to herself it was a vexed look, or a nice look. She had no name in her mind to pin it down, because it was a different look.

Mike himself could not have interpreted his feelings on hearing Mary Ann make her request ... irritation, disappointment, a touch of the old anger, and, covering all, a feeling of anticipated loneliness filled his mind. He thought, Something like this would have to happen.

He had said weakly, 'But why do you want to go, we are going into the farmhouse?'

This alone he had felt should have been attraction enough, affording her something to brag about for months to come; but her answer was, 'Yes, I know, but I ... well, I want to go to school ... and ... and talk nice.'

'And talk nice?' The old revolutionary in him was up in arms for the moment, and then he thought: It's a chance; who am I to deprive her of it? If I'd had it things might have been different. But as he looked at her he couldn't imagine any school being such an inducement that it could compete with himself.

His eyes slowly narrowed and his head lifted, and he asked quietly, 'Has Mr. Lord been talking to you?'

Her eyes had opened wide, and she had replied, 'Mr. Lord talking to me? What about?'

'You know,' he said, 'going to school.'

Now Mary Ann had lied for him all her life, but she had never been able to lie to him. Something in his eye always brought the truth out of her; it was as if she had no power to be other than what he demanded. But now, with the intuition born of her love, she knew from his odd quietness and the look on his face that Mr. Lord was right – if her da should guess she was going to school in exchange for his job he would get into a rage and everything would be spoilt. She could see him going to Mr. Lord and their fighting; and the result would be misery for them all again. So she cocked her head on one side and gave the first conscious acting performance of her life.

'Only when he was in the kitchen that day,' she said, 'and he mightn't send me now, but you could ask him. ... Will you, da? 'Cos you're always on to me about fighting, and I can't stop fighting where Sarah Flannigan is. She's always at me. And I'd like to talk nice, and show her.'

Mike's eyes were back to their normal roundness, and he turned towards the fire, saying, 'Go on now, we'll see about it later.'

She had gone out, but her ma had followed her to the gate, and there she had buttoned up her coat; then she had kissed her, a hard kiss, pressing her tightly. The kiss was not the usual morning peck, and it sent Mary Ann down the lane thinking, not of her da and his reactions, because she knew that he had believed her, but of her ma.

Before telling her mother that her teacher required a note to say she had been sick on the particular morning she had played truant, Mary Ann had informed her that she hadn't been to school but had gone to Mrs. McBride's, the excuse she gave being that it was dictation morning and she couldn't do dictation, and also that she was afraid of Miss Thompson. As both these statements in a way were true, she had not felt so bad about lying to her mother, but Lizzie had looked at her long and hard and, to her surprise, had not reprimanded her in any way, only tucked her in bed and said good night. She had put this lenient attitude down to her ma's joy at the turn of events. Yet now she wasn't sure, for her ma had said to her the next morning, 'Mind, say nothing to your da about staying off school and going to Mrs. McBride's.' And she had said 'All right', and thought: Just as if I would.

All told, she was finding the whole business disappointing. There was no excitement about it, only the excitement of knowing that she was acting, and that Mr. Lord knew she was acting. So the conclusion was reached that she was destined to become an actress, after first, of course, becoming a lady at that school.

Miss Thompson's voice exclaiming, 'All you for Confession,' brought the future bang into the present. She had forgotten about Confession. . . . Bust! And it'd be Father Beaney. And if she talked too much, he'd blow her up. Well, she decided firmly, she wasn't going to him. She'd march with the rest, go in and pay a visit, say a 'Hail Mary' for Father Owen, then go and see how he was.

But alas, there was still Miss Thompson to be reckoned with. Under that teacher's gimlet eye, it was quite impossible to carry out her plan, and in due course she found herself kneeling outside Father Beaney's box and wishing that she was ten miles away, or that he was. Her preparation for Confession was orthodox, but not her entry into the box; for she went in in a spirit of defiance. Yet she emerged, as one should, chastened; she had made so many promises she couldn't see them being fulfilled until she was an old woman. Oh, Father Beaney . . . he got on your nerves; he wasn't a bit like Father Owen. Fancy him saying she must stop ro . . . romancing . . . she didn't do that, she only made on about things. And she'd had to promise that she wouldn't fight any more, either with her tongue or hands, and that she would love her grannie . . . Well!

In a state of very mixed feelings she made her way to the altar of the Holy Family, and there she said her prescribed penance. It was no use, she knew, getting on about Father Beaney to them, for she could see by the look in their eyes they were on his side. She'd only get the worst of it. She next prayed for Father Owen. 'Make his cough better,' she asked them. 'And let him come out again; or let me in, 'cos I want to talk to him and tell him all that's happened. And thank you, dear Holy Family, for making all these fine things happen to us, especially to me da.' The gifts she had received from their hands made her contrite, and she added, 'I'll try to be a better girl, like Father Beaney said, and not fight with Sarah Flannagan ever again, or swank to her; and if I do, may I be struck down dead.' There! She felt that that spirit of sacrifice should please them. 'And dear Holy Family, will you make Miss Honeysett let me in so as I can see Father Owen? Glory be to the Father and to the Son, and to the

Holy Ghost. Amen. Oh' – she was almost off her knees – 'there's just one more thing ... me grannie. She won't come near us now, 'cos she knows everything's all right. But will you make me ma send me down to her so's I can tell the old ... her ... me grannie, all about everything?' Here she paused, and, when by neither sign nor feeling an answer came to her, she concluded that they weren't in favour of this request.

As if before some gentle rebuke, her head drooped, and she said dejectedly, 'But it's no use, I can't love her. You know yourself what she's like.'

Was it the sound of a chuckle that brought her head up? Well, it was something; and there, lo and behold, the whole lot of them were smiling. They were laughing about her grannie – they knew what she was like all right, better'n Father Beaney.

She rose from her knees, genuflected deeply, smiled broadly up at them; then, on reverent tip-toe, she went up the aisle and to the door leading to the porch. Here she stood for a moment, wallowing in her holy feeling and pulling on her woollen gloves. Then she straightened her hat, for she must be tidy if she was to meet Father Owen. Dusting down the front of her coat, she slowly made her way up the porch, but before she reached the door she was checked by a voice, low but audible, coming from the street outside, saying, 'Eeh! it's a wonder God doesn't strike her down dead. Me ma says that one of these days the heat from the devil in her will set light to the confessional box and she'll go up in blue smoke. D'you know what she's saying now – she's saying her da's been made manager and that she's going to be sent to a posh school and be made into a lady. Did you ever!' The voice rose: 'Her! ... Me ma says you can't make a silk purse out of a sow's ear, she says. ...'

Mary Ann had heard enough. ... Silk purse out of sow's ear! She wasn't exactly sure of the meaning of this saying, but that it reflected detrimentally on her she was sure. So she took three majestic steps out of the porch and confronted Sarah and her solitary listener, and startled them both by exclaiming, 'You can tell your ma you can make a silk purse out of a sow's ear, so there! What does your ma know anyway?'

Sarah, casting one devotional glance down the church porch, hissed quietly, 'You're starting again, and you're asking for it, and if we weren't near the church I'd give it to you.'

'You'll give me nothing,' said Mary Ann, 'that I won't give you back. And I am going away to a posh school, me ma came this morning, you saw her.'

'I saw her come because you got wrong for not bringing Miss Thompson a note, and you couldn't ask your ma for it, 'cos she didn't know you were playing truant.'

'It wasn't, you see; I had brought the note. . . . Oh! . . .' Mary Ann's eyes slowly mounted the grey stone of the church and reached the heavens; then descending earthwards again and seeming to have received a celestial message, she said with aloof dignity, 'It's no use talking to you. As me da says, some folks is born numbskulls and some fall on their heads.'

With this parting shot Mary Ann marched off, filled with a righteous feeling. She'd got the better of that do and she hadn't fought in the street.

Sarah's 'Oh . . . oh!' followed her, and she had not gone more than a few steps before Sarah's footsteps were behind her. Expecting at least a dig in the back and knowing that she would be forced to retaliate, she fled from temptation by spurting the few extra steps to the sanctuary of the priest's front-door step, and, without waiting to turn round, rang the bell.

This action alone stayed Sarah's hand – the daring of this enemy of hers had at times the power to bring on a stillness akin to paralysis. She stood now stock still, gaping at Mary Ann, who had the temerity to knock on the priest's front door, and him bad!

The door was opened and Miss Honeysett, looking like a replica of the avenging angel, stood there.

'Well?' she said.

'Can I see Father Owen, please?' asked Mary Ann in a small voice.

'No,' she said.

'Oh; is he worse then?'

'No,' she said.

'Is he up then?'

'Yes,' she said.

'And is he out and about?'

'No, he's not, he's not out of his room. And I'm sick of answering this door.'

'My name's Mary Ann Shaughnessy,' said Mary Ann in her politest tones, 'and if you told him it's me he'd let me in.'

Now Miss Honeysett became the avenging angel himself; she swelled, and wrath emanated from her. 'He would not! nor is he going to see anyone for days. You'd kill him, the lot of you. And don't come back botherin'.'

The door banged. There was a loud snigger from behind, and Sarah, her face wide with glee, said, 'Can I see Father Owen, because I'm the great Mary Ann Shaughnessy? And I'm going to a fine school, and me da' as manager ... poloney!'

Mary Ann, stumped for the moment, could only retort:

'Aw, you! you think you're clever. I'll get me own back on you, you wait.'

'Huh!' said Sarah, grinning from ear to ear. 'The only way you'll get your own back is when you spit in the wind.'

At this utter vulgarity, Mary Ann tossed her head and moved off until she came to the alleyway leading to the presbytery back yard. Here an idea struck her, and, turning to Sarah, she gave one emphatic bounce of her head, gathered up some gravel from the gutter, which action caused Sarah to duck, then marched disdainfully up the alleyway.

Father Owen had had a very trying day, during which the theory of loving his neighbour, in the person of his housekeeper, had been severely put to the test. For as many years as he could remember she had been trying to nurse him; in fact, he suspected her of praying illness on him. And now her prayer in some measure had been answered, and she had him where she wanted him. ... But for very little longer; tomorrow he was out of this, if he had to shoot his way out. He smiled wryly at the picture of himself, two guns at his hips, shooting at Miss Honeysett. God forgive him, she was a good woman – if only she didn't fuss.

He looked towards the window. Well, he supposed he

should be thankful. It was a grey day and the March wind had a nip in it, and here he was with a nice fire and a comfortable chair. What had he to grumble about? What? He lay back and closed his eyes, and was soon dozing. And now his dreams began to repay him for all the trials of the day and his life in general, for had he not here, in his very hand, an envelope with three thousand pounds in it, and not a word whom it was from, except to say it was for the restoration of his church? And Jimmy Connolly, him who was known never to have put more than a penny on the plate, and not that if he could get off with it, Jimmy had left six ounces of the best baccy together with a bottle of the finest Scotch on the doorstep, with the written injunction to take a good stiff dose of the latter to ward off a cold. ... Oh, the kindness of people. You'd never think, never dream. Under the skin they were all kind.

It was at this point of Father Owen's dream, and for no reason whatever that he could see, except perhaps for the unpredictability of human nature, that Jimmy Connolly fired a gun at him; from the vantage point of the outhouse roof, he fired at him, clean through the window.

'In the name of God!' Father Owen sat bolt upright in his chair. The noise of the gunshot was so realistic that it took some seconds for him to realize that he had been dreaming. He pushed his hands through his thinning strands of hair. He had been dreaming all right ... six ounces of baccy and a bottle of Scotch! Not forgetting the three thousand, of course. With a muttered exclamation of impatience he made to lean back again, when he was almost brought clean out of the chair by a loud 'Ping! ping!' on the window and as near resembling the crack of a gun as to be one.

'Glory be! Somebody throwing stones at the pane.'

Pulling himself up, he went to the window and peered down into the yard. But he could see no sign of the culprit, until a waving arm, coming from the end of the passage a little to the right of him, brought his eyes to Mary Ann.

Oh, it was Mary Ann. The child had come to see him. Well, well. He smiled and waved to her. What was she saying? With a stealthy glance behind towards the bedroom door and pulling the neck of his dressing-gown well up about his chin, he opened the window.

'Hallo, there, Mary Ann.'

'Hallo, Father. Are you better?'

'Right as rain.'

'I've been trying to see you for ages, and she wouldn't let me in.'

'She wouldn't?'

'No.'

'Just wait till I see her, she'll get the length of me tongue.' This whisper just reached Mary Ann, and that was all. She leant her head back now and whispered up hoarsely to him, 'A lot's happened, Father; I've piles to tell you.'

'Go on then, tell me.'

'Well, you know what you said about me da being manager?'

'Yes, I do, well enough.'

'Well, he is. Mr. Lord's made him the manager.'

Now Father Owen's surprise was genuine and his tone so full of awe that Mary Ann was filled with gratification.

'You don't say!' he said.

'Yes, and we're moving into the farmhouse.'

Father Owen stared down at the child. She was a modern miracle factory if ever there was one.... Old Lord to do that ... And why not, at all? It was the power of God working in him. And not before time.

'And you know something else, Father?'

'No ... tell me.'

Before Mary Ann told him she sent a swift glance down the alleyway and her voice became a number of tones higher. 'He's sending me to a posh school.'

'He's not!'

'He is ... a convent.'

'No!'

'Yes ... And you know some more?'

'No ... go on.'

'I'm goin' to be a lady and go on the pictures.'

'Glory be to God!' said Father Owen.

'And,' went on Mary Ann, remembering Sarah's saying which coupled the farmyard and the bag industry with herself, 'Sarah Flannagan says, Father, that I'll not, she says you can't make a silk purse out of a sow's ear.'

'Nonsense!' cried the priest. And then again, 'Nonsense!

You tell her from me you can; for was not I meself modelled
out of one?'

'You were, Father?'

'I was . . . I was indeed.'

'There you are then,' said Mary Ann loudly to the world
at large. 'And won't me da be a gentleman, Father?'

Father Owen was not called upon to sin his soul further,
for a voice from behind him crying, 'Father!' brought his
head in, and with a hasty wave and a wink to her he was
gone.

Glowing now with triumph Mary Ann sped down the alleyway, and just in time to stay Sarah's ignominious flight.
With the width of the pavement between them they confronted one another. A swarm of cutting remarks were tumbling over each other in Mary Ann's mouth, some fancifully
embellished, some flowery, and some just plain statements of
fact, but something in Sarah's face checked their flow and
they stuck between her teeth; and to her profound amazement and horror, she found herself actually feeling sorry for
this dire enemy, so much so that she almost contemplated
going off without a word. It was the most disconcerting feeling she had experienced in the whole of her life; and was not
under any circumstances to be encouraged, for should she go
off without some pithy remark Sarah would think she had
gone soft and would yell after her. And nobody, least of all
Sarah Flannagan, was going to think that she had gone soft.
So gathering all the remarks, fancy, flowery and plain, she
tied them together and delivered them as a bouquet:

'Spit against the wind yourself!' she said, and marched off
. . . unmolested.

Do you believe all about everything now? You don't?
Well, it'll serve you right if nothing nice ever happens to
you; it will so.

A SELECTED LIST OF
CATHERINE COOKSON TITLES
AVAILABLE FROM CORGI BOOKS

THE PRICES SHOWN BELOW WERE CORRECT AT THE TIME OF GOING TO PRESS. HOWEVER TRANSWORLD PUBLISHERS RESERVE THE RIGHT TO SHOW NEW RETAIL PRICES ON COVERS WHICH MAY DIFFER FROM THOSE PREVIOUSLY ADVERTISED IN THE TEXT OR ELSEWHERE.

□	13016 8	BILL BAILEY	£2.95
□	13274 8	BILL BAILEY'S LOT	£2.99
□	12473 7	THE BLACK VELVET GOWN	£3.99
□	11160 0	THE CINDER PATH	£2.95
□	12551 2	A DINNER OF HERBS	£3.99
□	10450 7	THE GAMBLING MAN	£2.95
□	10916 9	THE GIRL	£2.99
□	12789 2	HAROLD	£2.95
□	12608 X	GOODBYE HAMILTON	£2.99
□	12451 6	HAMILTON	£2.95
□	10267 9	THE INVISIBLE CORD	£2.95
□	09720 9	THE MALLEN STREAK	£2.75
□	09896 5	THE MALLEN GIRL	£2.95
□	10151 6	THE MALLEN LITTER	£2.95
□	11350 6	THE MAN WHO CRIED	£2.99
□	12524 5	THE MOTH	£3.50
□	13088 5	THE PARSON'S DAUGHTER	£3.95
□	10630 5	THE TIDE OF LIFE	£3.95
□	11737 4	TILLY TROTTER	£3.50
□	11960 1	TILLY TROTTER WED	£2.95
□	12200 9	TILLY TROTTER WIDOWED	£2.99
□	12368 4	THE WHIP	£3.99
□	10780 8	THE IRON FAÇADE (Catherine Marchant)	£1.95
□	10321 7	MISS MARTHA MARY CRAWFORD (Catherine Marchant)	£2.99
□	10541 4	THE SLOW AWAKENING (Catherine Marchant)	£2.99
□	13126 4	CATHERINE COOKSON COUNTRY (LF)	£5.95
□	01566 5	LET ME MAKE MYSELF PLAIN (Hardback)	£12.95

All Corgi/Bantam Books are available at your bookshop or newsagent, or can be ordered from the following address:

Corgi/Bantam Books,
Cash Sales Department,
P.O. Box 11, Falmouth, Cornwall TR10 9EN

Please send a cheque or postal order (no currency) and allow 60p for postage and packing for the first book plus 25p for the second book and 15p for each additional book ordered up to a maximum charge of £1.90 in UK.

B.F.P.O. customers please allow 60p for the first book, 25p for the second book plus 15p per copy for the next 7 books, thereafter 9p per book.

Overseas customers, including Eire, please allow £1.25 for postage and packing for the first book, 75p for the second book, and 28p for each subsequent title ordered.